Praise for
Baylor's Guide to Dreadful Dreams

"A ghostly good time."
—*Kirkus Reviews*

"Imfeld's wonderful imagination has spun
a story that is . . . quite fun."
—*Booklist*

**Check out Baylor's
first adventure**

Baylor's Guide to the Other Side

BAYLOR'S
Guide
to
Dreadful
Dreams

ROBERT IMFELD

Aladdin
New York   London   Toronto   Sydney   New Delhi

ALADDIN

An imprint of Simon & Schuster Children's Publishing Division
1230 Avenue of the Americas, New York, New York 10020
First Aladdin paperback edition September 2018
Text copyright © 2017 by Robert Imfeld
Cover illustration copyright © 2017 by Matt Saunders
Also available in an Aladdin hardcover edition.
All rights reserved, including the right of reproduction in whole or in part in any form.
ALADDIN and related logo are registered trademarks of Simon & Schuster, Inc.
For information about special discounts for bulk purchases, please contact
Simon & Schuster Special Sales at 1-866-506-1949 or business@simonandschuster.com.
The Simon & Schuster Speakers Bureau can bring authors to your live event.
For more information or to book an event, contact the Simon & Schuster Speakers Bureau
at 1-866-248-3049 or visit our website at www.simonspeakers.com.
Cover designed by Karin Paprocki
Interior designed by Mike Rosamilia
The text of this book was set in Centaur MT Std.
Manufactured in the United States of America 0818 OFF
2 4 6 8 10 9 7 5 3 1
The Library of Congress has cataloged the hardcover edition as follows:
Names: Imfeld, Robert, author.
Title: Baylor's guide to dreadful dreams / by Robert Imfeld.
Description: First Aladdin hardcover edition. | New York : Aladdin, 2017. |
Series: [A Beyond Baylor novel ; 2] | Summary: Aided by an amulet and his sister's ghost,
boy medium Baylor Bosco, thirteen, enters the world of dreams seeking two teens
lost at sea, while evading wandering demon spirits.
Identifiers: LCCN 2017002166| ISBN 9781481466394 (hc : alk. paper) |
ISBN 9781481466417 (eBook)
Subjects: | CYAC: Mediums—Fiction. | Ghosts—Fiction. | Brothers and sisters—Fiction. |
Missing persons—Fiction. | Demonology—Fiction. | Twins—Fiction. |
Mystery and detective stories. | BISAC: JUVENILE FICTION / Mysteries & Detective Stories.
| JUVENILE FICTION / Family / Siblings. | JUVENILE FICTION / Horror & Ghost Stories.
Classification: LCC PZ7.1.I4 Bay 2017 | DDC [Fic]—dc23
LC record available at https://lccn.loc.gov/2017002166
ISBN 9781481466400 (pbk)

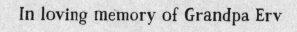

In loving memory of Grandpa Erv

BAYLOR'S
Guide to Dreadful Dreams

Keep your electronics away from ghosts.

BOY MEDIUM BAYLOR BOSCO: BEWITCHED OR BEDEVILED?

Keene, New Hampshire. A small town with a big claim to fame. Just last year, the annual Keene Pumpkin Festival achieved a Guinness world record for most jack-o'-lanterns gathered in one place—that's 30,581 pumpkins carved and lit up with candles.

In the last few weeks, however, the city has captured national attention for a *very* different reason.

Baylor Bosco, 13, claims to be a medium. A boy who, yes, talks to dead people.

Bosco first caught people's attention when he seriously injured a 68-year-old woman at a local Italian restaurant in early November.

"He was walking right toward her and sped up," said Michael Lindberg, who witnessed the incident. "She went flying to the ground. That little punk did it on purpose."

The paramedics were called, but strangely, no charges were filed. Witnesses reported that Bosco then held a group séance and communicated messages from patrons' "loved ones" for close to 30 minutes.

Less than a week later, Bosco was plastered all over the news again for his involvement in the disappearance of Winchester, NH, resident Rosalie Timmons. Ms. Timmons seriously injured herself after running full-speed into a vehicle that had blocked her path, according to the police report. And the driver of that vehicle? None other than Constance Bosco, the mother of the boy medium.

When asked about her role in Timmons's disappearance, Ms. Bosco emphatically uttered "No comment" no less than eight times while virtually running away from this intrepid reporter.

Baylor himself was a little more forthcoming. I was able to ask him questions during a recent walk home from school. The 13-year-old seems rather short for a boy his age; he has unstyled dirty blond hair, eyes the color of dirty lake water, and a permanent scowl stretched across his face.

"That woman was evil!" he screeched about Timmons, who had long been known in the Winchester community for her philanthropic efforts. "She tried to kill me!"

Then he appeared to have a spasm, as he grimaced at the air next to him and said, to no one, "No, Kristina, I'm not doing that." His clear affinity for inflicting pain onto others reared its ugly head when, a few moments later, he spouted off some deeply personal information about this reporter; information he'd clearly thoroughly researched before our meeting.

Whether Baylor Bosco does more good than harm with his supposed gift remains to be seen. Regardless, it looks as though Keene has another eccentric attraction here to stay.

—Carla Clunders, editor-at-large,

NewEnglandRealNews.net

I finished reading the article on my phone and sat dumbfounded on my bed. Rage tingled across my skin.

"Baylor, it's one bad article written by one terrible person," Kristina said, hovering over my shoulder. "Ignore it."

"Easy for you to say!" I scrolled through it again, trying to figure out which part was the worst.

"Isn't this the same website that picked a fight with the mayor and called him a 'really big doo-doo head'?"

"What's your point?"

"It's not exactly reputable. Think of all the nice articles about you that were posted on legitimate news sites. This woman is a fraud."

"I'm not short, Kristina, okay? I'm, like, five foot four. With shoes on, definitely five foot five."

"I didn't say you were short," she said slowly.

"Well, you didn't say I was tall, either," I said, glaring at her.

"I'm sorry, I didn't think I needed to considering how I've been saying for ten minutes that this woman is a moron," she said, her hands forming fists. "She's clearly a nonbeliever bent on making you look bad. Why are you wasting any energy on her?"

Somewhere deep down inside, I knew she was right. I mean, what kind of real journalist would compare someone's eyes to dirty lake water? (*Especially* when other people have compared those same eyes to a majestic spring sky, but that's beside the point.)

How could this woman sit there and write such negative things about me? What had I' ever done to her? Well, aside from delivering her dead sister's message about constipation solutions, but that was hardly my fault. It was, in the most literal sense, a healing message, and it was my life's purpose to deliver as many of them as possible.

I reread the line about spouting off some deeply personal information I'd researched before meeting her. Ha! She made it sound like we'd agreed to an interview when, in reality, she'd hopped out from behind a tree and ambushed me on my way home from school two days ago.

"Carla Clunders. What kind of stupid name is that anyway?"

"That's it, Baylor," Kristina said, her hand outlined

in blue. "No more." She wrapped her fingers around my phone and squeezed hard, emitting a pulse of blue energy; the screen went haywire.

"Did . . . did you just break my phone?"

She frowned, releasing her grip. "I really hope not, but I'm still getting used to this." She'd never been able to use any sort of energy before, but after my recent escapades battling some uninvited demon visitors, she'd finally gotten the go-ahead from . . . someone.

I still wasn't exactly sure how it worked with Kristina, my twin sister. She was miscarried in the womb, but somehow she grew up with me and hung around on the other side. She split her time between hanging with me and mingling with other ghosts in the Beyond, the place where all ghosts eventually wind up. The Beyond is sort of like an exclusive club on the other side, and only decent ghosts get admitted. There are other places and dimensions on the other side too, but unless you're a big fan of hordes of fiery-eyed demons, it's best to avoid those bad neighborhoods and stick to the Beyond.

She claims to go to the Beyond to learn lessons and get advice from spirit guides, but in my head, the Beyond was nothing more than one giant party, with a few billion ghosts just hanging out, sipping on some ghostly soda, eating some ghostly chips, for all of eternity. She always mentions chatting with all these iconic people, like Napoléon or Washington, but the only people I ever got to talk to were random dead people who wanted to tell their loved ones they needed to hit the gym. I wasn't jealous, per se—I like being alive, after all—but sometimes it felt like I was getting the short end of the stick.

Her long golden hair whipped around her face as she flexed her hand for a few seconds, wiggling her fingers. "I wonder if this is what it feels like, Baylor, when you lie on the couch for an hour watching TV and then your arm falls asleep and you whine about how much it tingles."

"You're not being helpful."

I glanced at the clock and sighed. I was going to be late for school if I didn't leave in exactly four minutes and speed walk the entire way. My day was already off to a bad start, and the last thing I needed was a detention on top of everything else.

I rushed through my morning routine—the usual stuff like brushing my teeth, combing my hair, and lighting candles to ward off evil spirits—and headed out the front door as Kristina chattered away in my ear.

"Think of all the positive news stories about you after the Rosalie incident. Why focus on the negative one?"

"It's just weird. It's almost like she's on a mission

to make me look bad. Isn't there some sort of law to protect me against creeps like her? I'm only thirteen, after all. She's endangering a child."

"You're acting a tad dramatic about this, don't you think?"

"No, I don't," I said. "In fact, I think I ought to sue Carla Clunders for libel."

Kristina rolled her eyes and muttered, "She wasn't wrong about the height thing."

I pretended like I didn't hear her and sped up. It was mid-November, and Keene was already experiencing frigid winter temperatures. I tried to convince my mom to drive me to school yesterday morning, but she laughed and said that the cold built character. I disagreed and told her walking a mile through freezing temperatures would only make me a bitter, unhappy person for the rest of my life, but she didn't seem too concerned about that.

By the time I got to school, my teeth were chattering like broken wind chimes.

"You look rough," Aiden said as I took my seat next to him. "Oversleep?"

"No," I said shortly. "I woke up to some stupid article written about me."

"Oh," he said, chuckling. "Another Bayliever blog post rambling on about how cute you are?"

My cheeks burned, but no longer because of the cold. "That was one time."

He shrugged. "Still. She had two hundred comments all agreeing with her. Another one's bound to pop up sooner or later."

"Well, this new one is the opposite of that. For some reason this woman is determined to make me look bad."

"Make you look bad?" J said, sitting in the desk in front of Aiden. "That's not exactly hard to do, Baylor." She winked at me through her neon-green glasses. J was so smart that if she didn't become one of the youngest astronauts ever, it'd only be because she was probably busy studying for medical and law degrees at the same time.

"Good morning to you, too, J," I said, scowling.

She turned to Aiden and smiled. "Morning!"

Aiden sputtered and choked on his own breath. Kristina and I looked at each other and shook our heads. They'd been going out for maybe ten days now—after Aiden finally got the nerve to tell her he liked her in a musical blaze of glory prompted by yours truly—but he somehow acted more nervous than ever around J.

"Anyway," J said, her eyes framed by the bright green glasses. "Are you guys ready for tomorrow?"

The band was marching in Keene's Thanksgiving Day Parade. I played the tuba; Aiden rocked the flute. The parade always takes place the Saturday before Thanksgiving because most of the residents head out of town for the holiday. Keene learned that lesson the hard way during its inaugural parade a few years ago, when it was held on Thursday morning and only, like, twenty people showed up to watch it.

"I think so," I said. "Now that Mr. G. finally dropped that weird "Silent Night/All I Want for Christmas Is You" mash-up, I think we're in pretty good shape."

She chuckled. "I'm bummed I never got to hear it."

Kristina groaned from behind. "She should consider herself lucky."

I agreed with Kristina. If I never heard any of those songs again, I'd be a happy guy. It wasn't just because the mash-up sounded like a chorus of dying parrots, though. It also brought up some bad memories from the last few weeks.

Right around Halloween, I'd been plagued by a demon wearing a sheet, whom I endearingly referred to as the Sheet Man. It turned out the demon was this poor dead guy named Alfred who was being controlled by his ex-wife, Rosalie. That wasn't so easy to figure out, though. At one point, I'd wound up in the hospital after the Sheet Man visited me during band practice. We'd been rehearsing the mash-up when he just showed up out of nowhere and, next thing I knew, I woke up in hospital, nearly concussed after my tuba had fallen on my head.

All's well that ends well, though, and that whole situation ended when Rosalie was suddenly picked off by a horribly evil spirit called a Bruton, one of the worst kinds of demons around, and taken to some place far, far away.

Okay, so maybe it didn't end well for Rosalie, but that's what happens when you involve yourself in evil activities.

After school, during the last rehearsal before the parade, Mr. G. made us run through the songs and practice our marching about a million times. By the time I got home, I was ready for a nap before dinner.

"Well, before you nap, I just want to warn you," Kristina said, her voice sounding a bit thin.

I turned to her slowly. Warnings from Kristina were just about my least favorite things in life. "What is it?"

"Well, it's nothing bad," she said quickly, looking sort of embarrassed, "but tonight we'll be having some company."

I glared. "Are you saying—?"

"Kristina! Baylor!" rang a British voice from behind me. "How are you this fine evening?"

Even ghosts adore
British accents. Ugh.

"COLONEL FLEETWOOD," I SAID THROUGH gritted teeth, my eyes tearing into Kristina's. "You're back."

I turned around to find a very young and very dead British soldier, immaculately dressed in a red coat. The colonel had dropped into my life a few weeks earlier when things were going rather poorly—again, the whole Sheet Man situation.

I thought the colonel would go away for good after that was resolved, but nope, he stuck around. He'd been gone the last few days so it seemed like I'd finally gotten rid of him, but here he was. Again.

"Feeling a bit chaffed, Baylor?" he said, taking note of my grimace. "A bad day at school?"

"Oh, just ignore him," Kristina said hastily, brushing past me with a chill. "Baylor's been mad all day because some hack journalist wrote a nasty article about him on her website."

"Her website," the colonel said slowly. "I know this one. That's a component of the marvelous Internet, right? Everyone's connected through the means of an invisible web, a different kind of worldwide web, and this *website* is her particular place in that system?"

"Sure," I said, shrugging carelessly. "Why not?"

The colonel smiled proudly and looked at Kristina. "I'm starting to catch on!"

"So," Kristina said, "did you figure it out?"

"Figure what out?" I asked.

"I did," he said. "Here's a surprise: It's simple."

"What's simple?" I asked.

"Oh, good. Is it what I thought it was?" she asked.

"What'd you think what was?" I asked.

"Shut up, Baylor, we're trying to help you here," Kristina said, exasperated.

I frowned. "You di——"

"Oh, there's that permanent scowl Carla mentioned!" Kristina said, pointing at my face as the colonel looked on in confusion.

Before I could think of anything clever to say back, Mom shouted "Dinner!" from downstairs.

"You'll pay for that one, Kristina Bosco."

Dinner that night was beef stew, and as my family and I sat around the table to eat, I had the distinct displeasure of having to watch Kristina and Colonel Fleetwood whispering to each other in the family room. I could only catch snippets of what they were saying over the clatter of my baby sister, Ella. She has more rolls on her little body than an Italian bread basket and a smile brighter than last month's full moon, but for a one-and-a-half-year-old, she could make some serious noise:

"Goo-la-la-BAH!" Ella shouted.

". . . stone . . ."

Bang bang bang. She was hitting her spoon on her feeding tray.

". . . Rosalie . . ."

"That's my smart girl," cooed my mom as Ella lathered herself with mashed peas.

". . . amulet . . ."

Just as Ella started shrieking, I couldn't take it anymore.

"Will you stop?" I shouted at her. She looked at me, scared, and started to cry. Everyone went quiet, including Kristina and the colonel.

"Baylor," my mom said calmly. "Is there a reason you're screaming at the baby?"

I flushed. "I . . . I didn't mean to. I'm just frustrated."

"And why are you frustrated?"

"Because."

"Oh, really? *Because?*" she said, nodding sarcastically. "That's how you're going to answer me? You want to rethink that?"

"It involves ghost stuff," I said. "You wouldn't like it."

Jack, my little brother, dropped his spoon and shivered, while my dad concentrated hard on his stew, foraging for the right vegetable-to-meat ratio.

"Don't try to pull the 'ghost stuff' line on me, young man," she said with a dry laugh. "It won't work anymore. That ship has sailed."

Until recently, that line would have put a stop to the conversation. She'd been feeling less afraid of *ghost stuff*, though, after seeing Rosalie flying unnaturally through the air, shrieking hysterically as the Bruton carried her off. I could see the Bruton carrying her, but my mom could only see some helpless woman soaring through the sky, her legs askew, her arms flailing wildly, with as much dignity as a rat caught in talons of an eagle.

"I actually just think I'm irritated by that article that got released about me," I said with a shrug. I didn't want to name-drop Kristina or the colonel when I didn't even know what they were discussing.

"What article?" my mom asked, her eyes narrowing.

"From that *New England Real News* website. You were actually mentioned in it," I said. "The writer sort of made it seem like we'd plotted together to hurt Rosalie."

Her eyebrows shot up, and she looked around the table. "*New England Real News?* Please tell me that's not the one that did a five-part investigative series trying to prove that vegetables are actually bad for you."

I nodded grimly.

"Everyone done with dinner?" she asked, her eyes already darting in the direction of the office, where she could pull up the article on the computer. I'd barely touched my stew, and Dad and Jack weren't even halfway through their bowls. "Good, good. I'm just going to . . . " She got up and half ran to the office.

"May I be excused?" I asked Dad, who nodded half-heartedly.

"Might as well," he said, dropping his spoon into the bowl. "Sounds like your mother's going to be occupied for a while."

"Fantastic," I said, getting up and turning to the ghosts. "Kristina, Colonel—upstairs, now!"

Ella, who had already recovered from my outburst, turned to the colonel and shrieked. "Flee Flee Flee!" Ella, like most babies, could see spirits. She'd grow out of it one day, but for now, she was just another female Bosco who was obsessed with the colonel.

"My beautiful Ella," the colonel cooed, rushing over to place his hand on her cheek. "How are you, lovely?" She laughed and smacked her cheek a few times, and I rolled my eyes.

"Gross," I muttered. "Let's go."

Back in my room, I sat on my bed as I listened to them rehash what they'd been talking about.

"We knew after the Bruton fiasco with Rosalie that we needed to strengthen our protections. Candles are great, but they're not cutting it on their own any-more."

"So you guys came up with something new?"

Colonel Fleetwood was distracted by the photo-graphs clustered together on the bookcase by the window. He was leaning in, carefully studying each one.

"We did," Kristina said. "We've worked with our spirit guides on the best way to proceed, and Colonel Fleetwood finally got an actionable answer tonight."

"Actionable?"

"We can do a lot on our end," Kristina said, "but it's even better when you can establish a physical protection to cordon yourself off from harm."

I had a flashback to the Bruton surrounding us with fire in Rosalie's basement—the intense heat from the fire that took the shape of people writhing in pain, the desperation on Kristina's face as she tried to put out the flames, the mind-numbing fear that pulsed through my body as I realized I was about to die.

"Yeah, that sounds good to me," I said brightly. "So what do I need to do?"

Kristina turned to the colonel, who was examining an old photo of Grandpa Bosco and me. He'd died years before. "Colonel Fleetwood?"

The colonel perked up, startled. "Apologies! I was distracted by the charming photo of Baylor and Douglas."

"Douglas? You call Grandpa Bosco by his first name?"

"Well, of course," he said, sounding confused. "He's not my grandfather, after all."

"Yeah, but still . . . it's weird."

In all honestly, I was jealous he got to see my grandpa. He said his name so nonchalantly, too, as though he and his ol' pal Douglas hung out all the time in the Beyond, telling each other jokes and goofing around and having the best time ever. What a jerk.

"Anyway," Kristina continued, "Colonel Fleetwood, if you'd like to explain your news?"

"Indeed!" he said. "Baylor, we're enhancing your protection, and it's really quite simple."

"Do share, then, old chap!"

"Baylor," Kristina said, her face in her hand, "why?"

The colonel pressed on. "The stone, the one you made for the talisman to defeat the Sheet Man? Its power remains, and we can harness it to protect you."

I frowned, leaning over to my nightstand to retrieve the stone from one of the drawers. The first night I met the colonel, I had to go hunting for materials to make a talisman, an object that wards off evil spirits. I needed a piece of wood, a round stone, and an egg, and we somehow ghost-rigged the stone inside the egg and sealed it shut. I'd eventually cracked it open and used the stone to stop Rosalie and the Sheet Man.

Afterward, I'd discreetly picked it up from Rosalie's house when we stopped by with the police after the Bruton incident. I'd kept it as a souvenir of sorts, as weird as that may sound, but it was easier to hold on to than either the cracked eggshells that had encased it or the primitive wooden bowl I'd spent hours whittling.

"This thing?" I asked. "It's just a rock."

"Just a rock?" Kristina scoffed. "It was able to break the negative energy that bound the Sheet Man, remember?"

"Yeah," I scoffed back. "That one time, after we had done the magical thingamajig with the lights and the chanting."

Kristina smiled slyly. "There's more where that came from."

Amulets: Good for keeping bad spirits away, but bad for blending in.

"NO," I SAID. "ABSOLUTELY NOT."

"Why not?" Kristina asked. "It's for your own good!"

She and Colonel Fleetwood had just explained what they wanted me to do with the stone, and since it involved wearing it like a necklace, it wasn't going to work out.

"Because guys my age don't wear necklaces," I said. "Jared Terrance came back from a trip to Hawaii wearing a puka shell necklace, and everyone destroyed him for it. He had to take three fake sick days in a row just to get people to forget about it!"

"This is going to be a lot different than a puka shell necklace, Baylor."

"You're right," I said, nodding fervently. "It's going to be a whole lot worse, because that stone is big and bulky, and there's no way I'm going to be able to hide it. People are going to notice it instantly. I'll have to admit I'm wearing some weird stone necklace under my shirt because the only alternative is saying I have an alien parasite growing out of my chest."

Kristina crossed her arms and tapped her foot impatiently. "You know how this is going to end, right? You're going to keep complaining, and Colonel Fleetwood and I are going to sit here and listen; finally, once you wear yourself out, you're going to give in and do it. So, in the interest of time, can we just skip to the last step?"

"You think you know me so well," I said, annoyed that she was probably right. "Well, guess what?"

"What?" she said, in mock surprise. "Are you suddenly not going to give in? Are you going to act like a headstrong idiot for a few more days before you realize how stupid you're being and finally agree to do what we wanted you to from the beginning, but you'll feel better about yourself because you at least stood your ground?"

We glared at each other in silence for a few

moments while the colonel politely studied the popcorn ceiling.

"Let's just get this over with," I finally said.

I'd originally found the stone and wood for the talisman on the night of a full moon, and the three of us had used our energy to create it from that. Thankfully, since the weird mystical stuff was already accounted for, the process of making the necklace was fairly painless. I took some twine from my dad's workspace in the basement and wrapped a long piece around the stone a bunch of times. Then I looped a different piece through the twine and tied it together to form the most primitive necklace I'd ever seen. It looked like something a caveman would give to his cavewife as an anniversary gift.

"My one request," I said, examining the creation in my hands, "is that we don't call it a necklace."

"It's really more of an amulet," Colonel Fleetwood said.

"I'm not sure that's better," I said, scrunching my eyebrows together.

"We'll figure the wording out later," Kristina said gently. "We need to finalize the protections on it."

"More weird bands of light coming from our fingers?" I asked, remembering the bizarre tornado of energy that we'd somehow conjured to create the original talisman.

"Nope," Kristina said. "Fire. Lots and lots of fire. Light your candle."

I stockpiled candles the way other thirteen-year-olds stockpile baseball cards, and I always had a few scattered throughout my room. I lit one every morning so the fire's energy could surround me and keep me safe. I did as Kristina asked and set the lit candle on the desk in front of me.

"Good. You'll need to do two things now."

"The first," the colonel said, "is to memorize this line: *Surround me with white light and protect me in the dark night.*"

"Simple enough," I said. "What's the second thing?"

"As you're saying that line, you'll have to dip the amulet into the candle's flame," Kristina said.

"Won't that burn the twine? And make it useless?"

"Not if you don't screw it up."

So I did as they instructed. I said the lines aloud (and then, for good measure, repeated them over and over again in my head), and brought the amulet down to the flame. It took several seconds for the brown, itchy twine to catch fire, but once it did, it burned with intensity—the flame seemed to alternate between gold and blue, and it hissed in an oddly satisfying way.

I had a moment of panic when I realized the flame was about to inch its way up to where my fingers were holding the amulet. Kristina noticed, and she reached out her hands and held mine. I couldn't feel them, but a chill lingered around my fingers.

"Trust us," she whispered. And sure enough, the flame licked up and around my hands, but it didn't burn my skin. After a few more seconds of burning and hissing, the flame snuffed itself out with a dramatic *poof*.

The amulet had transformed. The brown, itchy twine was now smooth and dark, almost like leather. The stone had morphed from perfectly white to an ashy silver, and it wasn't as bulky, like it had shed a layer or two of stone.

"Nice," I said in a hushed voice. I put it around my neck and under my shirt, and for a moment, the glassy stone burned hot against my skin. I grabbed it off my chest, but in my hand, the stone felt cool.

"And that's all there is to it!" Kristina said. She and the colonel smiled at each other.

"So what does it do?" I asked. "I'm protected against everything now?"

The colonel laughed. "If only it were that easy.

This is just an enhancement to your protections. Should you find yourself swarmed by evil spirits, the amulet will offer enough protection to fend off attacks to your body and spirit."

"Wouldn't it be better if it could keep me from getting swarmed by evil spirits in the first place?"

"One step at a time, Baylor," Kristina said. "We're working on it."

"Right," I said warily. "Better than nothing, I guess."

I keep a dream journal on my nightstand in case I get any weird messages in the middle of the night, mostly from the little kids who sometimes rush through my dreams. It's a woefully ineffective way of communicating a message since scribbling in the dark while half asleep isn't simple, and I'll often wind up staring at the words for a while trying to decipher their meaning. It doesn't happen often, though, mainly because ghosts don't really bother me in my dreams, and if they do, I can usually remember the message.

Anyway, I'm only supposed to be able to communicate with ghosts whose loved ones are in my proximity, so I shouldn't be getting any random messages unless someone is hiding out in my closet in the middle of the night. And if that turned out to be the case, I'd have bigger problems than some incomprehensible messages.

That night, I drifted off into one of the strangest sleeps I've had in a while. At first I didn't even realize I was asleep. I was in band rehearsal, and Mr. G. said he'd not only given up on the Christmas mash-up for the Thanksgiving Day Parade, but he'd also given up on us completely.

"I've decided to quit my job and become a ski instructor in Argentina," he announced to the room of stunned faces, his long, golden-red hair shining brightly from an invisible source of light somewhere behind him. "I figure I can't be any worse at that than I am at this job."

"But—but have you ever skied before?" asked my friend Bobby, who was slumped over his drum, devastated.

"Sure haven't," he said.

"Well, that doesn't seem like a good idea."

"You're right," I said, turning to Bobby. And he was. Mr. G. wouldn't just abandon ship in such a grand way. In that moment, it dawned on me I was dreaming, and it was like a hazy veil had been lifted from my eyes. I looked around the room and a few things affirmed my realization.

First off, Aiden was weeping into his flute, and

although I wouldn't be shocked if Aiden actually *did* cry at this kind of news, I doubted his tears would rival the intensity of a small waterfall. Next, I looked at the sheet music in front of me, but the musical notes were just doodles of cats. Finally, I spotted a giant, bulbous octopus in the corner of the room, its tentacles stirring limply as it attempted to grasp its slippery saxophone. That pretty much sealed the deal for me.

Mr. G. had somehow changed into brightly colored ski clothes and was clutching a pair of skis in one hand and poles in the other.

"Time to go!" he said, heading to the door.

"I'll join you," I said, and stood up to follow him out of the room.

"Argentina's a long way away, Baylor," Mr. G. said as he sauntered outside. "Are you sure your parents will . . ."

But then he faded away, and I found myself in a vast black room, as if I'd accidentally launched myself into outer space. It was warm and cozy, as though I were wrapped in the most luxurious blanket money could buy. A pathway stretching left and right sprawled out as far I could see; the ground was illuminated by what looked like shimmering shooting stars. Some were brighter than others, and I was standing on one tinged with a blue glow.

I half walked, half floated to the left, wondering what to do. Billions of stars filled the vast space around me, glowing warmly despite their distance. At my feet, stars were spaced evenly apart down either side of the pathway; it looked vaguely like an airport runway, but it felt more like a universe that belonged just to me. One particular shooting star was flashing intensely a few feet away from where I'd entered. I was curious as to what would happen if I stepped onto it. I placed a foot on it, and with a soft *whoosh*, I somersaulted forward and gently tumbled into a rolling field.

The sun was setting behind massive oak trees on a hill in the distance; the sky was ablaze with vivid stripes of various shades of pink, blue, and gold, like someone had spilled paint all over a canvas and mixed all the colors together.

I walked down the hill, gazing in awe at the sky, and stumbled into Bobby again. He was sitting cross-legged on a picnic blanket, drinking a cup of tea, while a moose sat across from him, also cross-legged and drinking from a matching, but slightly larger teacup. On a fancy platter in front of them were two kinds of ants-on-a-log: the celery, peanut butter, and raisin version for Bobby, and an actual log crawling with ants for the moose.

Even though Bobby was one of my good friends and probably the goofiest person I knew, I'd never dreamed about him twice in a night before. It didn't entirely surprise me that I'd dream up such a weird scenario for him.

"Baylor!" Bobby exclaimed. "Hey, dude! Nice of you to join!"

"Thanks, Bobby," I said, laughing. "Who's your friend?"

"Mr. Moose is an old acquaintance of mine," Bobby said. Then, in what looked like a move they'd rehearsed many times, they reached behind their backs, pulled out top hats, put them on their heads, and nodded toward me.

I had never seen a moose move so gracefully—that thing was huge, and for it to balance the top hat on its antlers was impressive. I was strangely jealous of their hats.

"Do you have a spare for me? I'd hate to look underdressed for the party."

"But of course," said Bobby, and he motioned to the moose, which reached into a raccoon-fur satchel and pulled out another hat for me.

"Thank you," I said, the top hat fitting snuggly on my head.

"Snack?" Bobby asked.

"No thanks," I said, "I don't love raisins."

"Who does? Those are for Mr. Moose," Bobby said, picking up the log. "We get the ants." He shoved the log against his mouth and licked voraciously.

I gawked at him. "That's really gross, Bobby."

He frowned, still chewing. "Ever tried them?" he asked between bites as little bits of ant legs and guts splattered out of his mouth.

"I can't say I have," I said.

"Don't knock it till you try it."

The moose shook his head and reached for the celery.

"I think it's time to wake up," I said, turning around to see if there was some sort of door I could go through. There was nothing there. "But how do I get back?"

"Follow the light," Bobby said simply.

"How'd you know that?" I asked.

He shrugged. "It's my picnic."

As I got up, he reached for more ants from the log and the moose licked the celery clean of peanut butter and raisins. I walked up the hill, focusing on the sun in the distance, letting the beautiful sky absorb me and send me into a different dream I'd never remember.

TIP

4

Dreaming about
a fancy moose is
NOT normal.

WHEN I WOKE UP IT FELT LIKE ONLY TEN
minutes had passed since I'd fallen asleep. My dream
journal was empty, and Kristina was nowhere to be seen.
I wanted to talk to her about everything I'd dreamed.

"Kristina," I whispered in the dark. "Where are
you?"

"Here," she said, materializing onto my bed.
"Good morning to you."

"The weirdest thing happened to me last night."

Her face sunk. "Oh no. What happened? Was it
the amulet?"

"No, no, nothing like that," I said. "My dreams—they were so vivid. It was like I knew I was dreaming, and then I could sort of go into this weird black space and choose what I wanted to dream next. It was like a choose-your-own-adventure game."

Kristina nodded, her face stony. "Sounds like you had a lucid dream." She shrugged. "It's when you realize you're awake in the middle of a dream. Lots of people have them."

"Oh," I said, feeling a bit deflated. "I thought it had something to do with my gift since it seemed so real."

"That's an interesting thought."

"Apparently I don't think much of Bobby," I said. "I dreamed he was picnicking with a moose and eating ants."

She chuckled. "Sounds right to me."

A few hours later, Mr. G. was greeting the band members with donuts as we arrived downtown before the parade began.

I took a chocolate-frosted donut and was about to bite into it when I remembered my dream. "Hey, Mr. G., you ever been skiing?"

"Once, when I was younger. Broke my leg. Hated it ever since. Why do you ask, Baylor?"

"No reason," I said. "Glad to hear that."

"You're glad to hear I broke my leg?" he said, clucking his tongue at me. "Happy Thanksgiving to you, too!"

I made a face of mock horror and then walked with Kristina over to where Bobby and Aiden were standing with some of our other bandmates.

"Baylor, dude," Bobby said. "I had the most insane dream about you last night."

"Weird," I said, laughing. "I dreamed about you last night too!"

"I bet it wasn't as crazy as mine, though," he said, his eyes wide and eager. He took the marching cap off his head and ran his fingers through his buzzed hair. "I was in this field, right? And I was hanging out with this real fancy moose by the name of Mr. Moose, naturally, and we both had top hats, and then you showed up and wanted a top hat. And then I was eating ants for some reason, and you looked like you were about to vomit, and then you just sort of disappeared, and then the moose was mad at you for leaving abruptly so he started neighing like a horse." Bobby frowned. "But I think that's mainly because I'm not sure what noise a moose would make when it's angry."

He put the cap back on his head, adjusted it, and looked at me. "Weird, right? What was your dream?"

I knew I was still standing. I could feel my feet against the ground, and I could feel my fingers clasping the donut. But at that moment, my insides had turned to ice, my head felt very light, and my eyes were boring into Kristina's.

She didn't look nearly as concerned as I thought she should, though, and seemed far too interested in the clarinet players warming up.

"Baylor?" Bobby asked, looking concerned. "You there, bud?"

"Uh, er, yeah. Sorry," I said, my voice suddenly hoarse. "Didn't get much sleep."

"So what was your dream?" he asked.

"It was, uh, weird," I said, trying to conjure something in my mind besides a fancy moose and ant snacks. "Mr. G. was in it too, and he said he was moving to Argentina to become a ski instructor, and you and Aiden were really upset."

"Hmm," Bobby said, mulling it over. "That'd be kinda awesome."

I nodded. "I already checked—Mr. G. hates skiing."

For the next hour I kept trying to catch Kristina's eye, but she seemed suspiciously distracted that morning. Before I knew it, it was nearly ten o'clock, and we had to get lined up and ready to march.

We were near the end of the parade procession, though, so there was still more standing around and waiting to do.

"What is that hissing noise?" I mumbled to Kristina, screwing up my eyes and trying to block it out.

She'd decided to be communicative again, and her mouth was hanging half open in shock. "It's Clarinet Cassie's grandmother. Musical talent runs in their family, apparently. She's showing off her opera skills and hitting a note only ghost dogs can hear."

"Is that what the weird barking is too?"

She nodded. "You should tune in. It's fascinating." It'd taken years of practice, but I could tune spirits out by imagining the scene around me without them in it and letting that image become my reality. It was usually more pleasant and much quieter without the spirits, though the persistent ones could still break through my mental barrier.

"I'll pass," I said bitterly, wishing I could totally seal off the connection for a few minutes. "Are you planning to comment on Bobby's dream at all?"

"Oh, look, Mr. G.'s trying to get everyone's attention," she said, pointing forward.

I rolled my eyes. She could avoid me all she wanted for now, but I'd force her to talk to me tonight.

I was worried I was going to be distracted, that

the shock of Bobby's dream would disrupt my ability to tune ghosts out and I'd suddenly cause a ruckus in the middle of the parade. With so many people watching and who knows how many ghosts clamoring for a message to get delivered, it seemed all too possible.

Things went smoothly for the most part, but there was one close call. About ten minutes after we began marching, Clarinet Cassie's grandma finally broke through, and she began singing a message in the form of an *arpeggio*.

> *"Tell my dear Cassandra*
> *hard work's taken her far.*
> *She's come a long way*
> *and practiced so hard*
> *since smashing her mom's guitar."*

Needless to say, I completely lost my place in the melody, and I was suddenly ruining "Santa Claus Is Coming to Town" as people in the crowd grimaced at the off-key tuba.

Kristina shot a blast of blue energy at her, sending her back to the Beyond.

"Demon dung!" Kristina yelled, furious. "Why would she choose this moment to get you to deliver a message? Sorry, Baylor."

Aside from that hiccup, it was fun to spot some

familiar faces in the crowd. Reverend Henry was there with his family, and Madame Nadirah was standing outside of her shop, handing out promotional flyers to the passersby. I saw my family beaming at me from their spot near the downtown square. My grandparents waved at me excitedly, and even Aunt Hilda managed a proud nod.

After the parade ended, I evaded Mr. G.'s glares—he wouldn't get over my screw up for a few weeks—and found my family.

"My talented boy!" Mom said, holding up her phone to take a picture. "Smile, Baylor!"

Grandpa By (which we called him as an alternative to Byron O'Brien) stood next to her, beaming.

"Baylor O'Brien—" he said.

"It's Baylor *Bosco*," my dad said, annoyed, as he bounced Ella up and down.

"Baylor Bosco, you are one spectacular tuba player. I'm not trying to start any trouble, but I think we all know which side of the family you get your musical talent from." He pointed at his chest and winked as my dad shook his head. "I'm just saying."

"You don't even play an instrument, By," Dad said. "And you can't even hit the right notes when you sing 'Happy Birthday.'"

"That's a surprisingly hard song to sing, but what

does it matter, Doug? Let me tell you something, I have great taste in music, and it shows through my grandson." He nodded. "It shines through him, actually. It's an O'Brien trait, this great taste in music. It's something real special."

"What'd you think, Jack?" I asked my seven-year-old brother.

He wasn't paying attention, though. He was looking sideways at a group of kids I recognized from his class. There were five or six of them, mostly boys, standing in a circle and joking around with one another.

"Are those some of your friends, Jack?" I asked. He was such a quiet kid, and I honestly wasn't sure who his friends were. He rarely invited anyone over.

"Not really," he whispered.

"What do you mean 'not really'?" I asked. "You're in second grade. Everyone's friends with everyone in second grade."

He shrugged, and the big brother signal clicked on in my brain. Were these kids bullying him? I shot a look at Kristina, who also seemed to pick up on Jack's body language, and she narrowed her eyes.

Without thinking, I marched over to the group of kids.

"Baylor," Jack called after me, his voice trembling, "what are you doing?"

I ignored him. He could be nervous all he wanted; if these little punks were messing with my little brother, I was going to put a stop to it right now.

"What's up, guys?" I said to the group of kids. There were four boys and two girls, and when they looked up to see who was talking to them, their faces fell. I felt vindicated: They clearly knew I was Jack's big brother, and I was here to put them in their places for how they were treating him.

No one responded to my question, so I kept going.

"Listen, guys, I'm Jack's older brother, Baylor." I tried to make my voice a bit deeper.

"We know who you are," said a round-faced boy wearing a red beanie. I was pretty sure he was the little brother of a seventh-grader who was in the band with me. They had the same big, rosy cheeks.

"Good," I said. "I just wanted to make sure you guys are being cool to Jack."

Their blank, borderline-scared faces seemed like a bad sign to me.

"He's a friendly guy," I continued. "Maybe you could all hang out?"

Two of the boys looked at each other, grave concern in their eyes.

"Baylor," Kristina said, a note of surprise in her voice, "I don't think this is what you think it is."

But before I could respond, the kid in the beanie spoke up. "We like Jack."

"Oh," I said. "That's good. Then what's——?"

An old man with the kid's matching flushed cheeks popped up in front of me, sputtering incomprehensibly. I jumped in surprise and turned my head to glare at him.

"What are you doing?"

"Tell my grandson I miss him! Please. I know you were tuning us out, but I'm not going to have this chance for a while."

"Fine," I said. "No problem."

I turned back to the group of kids, but they were all now looking at me, mouths wide open, terrified.

Before I could say anything, the kid in the beanie yelled, "He's doing it!" At once, they all screamed and scrambled away.

I stood there, openmouthed, as adults turned my way and scorned me with their eyes. I looked back at Jack, whose expression suggested a bucket of ice water had been dumped on his head, then to my parents, who looked incredibly confused, and finally to Kristina.

"They're not bullying Jack," I said, the horrible realization still dawning on me. "They're scared of me."

"Demon dung," Kristina whispered. "How did we miss this?"

I had no response. Did Jack not have any friends because of me—or rather, us? How long had that been going on? Did Mom and Dad know?

I shuffled back over to him, my shoulders feeling heavy. "That went well!"

"Did it?" Dad asked, rocking Ella back and forth. "You wanted them to scream and run away from you?"

"What did you say to them, Baylor?" Mom asked.

"Probably scared them with some ghost stories," Aunt Hilda chimed in. I glared at her, annoyed that her contempt for my gift was justified for once.

"We were just kidding around," I said. "You should invite them to the house next week, Jack. I bet you'd have fun."

Jack shook his head. "That's okay, Baylor," he said, sounding so disappointed, like it was his birthday and his cake was actually a handful of twiggy mud.

But it wasn't okay. And I was going to fix it.

TIP

5

Make sure you get your shut-eye.

WE ALL ATE LUNCH AT TIO JUAN'S, OUR favorite Mexican place downtown, and I was feeling awfully full from an overload of enchiladas. Before I took a siesta, though, I needed to corner Kristina.

"Time to explain," I said once I'd crawled into bed.

"Baylor, really, there's nothing much to explain here," she said, sitting at the foot of my bed. "You visited Bobby's dream. And Ella's, too. It's not a big deal."

"You're kidding, right? It's not a big deal? It's a *huge* deal. I can enter people's minds, basically."

She rolled her eyes. "You're not entering their minds, Baylor. Believe me. You're just entering their dreams. It's very different."

"You're acting way too calm about this."

"Well, it's not a coincidence this happened the first night you wore the amulet. It's probably knocked down some kind of mental barrier now!"

"So I should stop wearing it then?" I asked, semi-hopeful. After we'd transformed the amulet, it wasn't as noticeable as I'd feared. Still, there was always a chance someone might notice it.

"What? No. Always wear it."

Not the answer I was looking for, but I had other pressing questions. "So I can walk into anyone's dreams?"

"Not just anyone," she said. "They have to be loved ones."

"But I shouldn't be able to just saunter into other people's dreams like that. It could be dangerous or something."

"You were perfectly safe. And do I need to remind you that you were the one who chose to go into their dreams? You could have stayed put in your own dreams."

"But . . . but . . . it feels wrong! It's intrusive."

"It is, but really, we shouldn't get into the intrusive conversation," Kristina said. "How many times have you gone up to strangers innocently going about their day to deliver a message from the other side?"

"That's different," I said.

"How?"

"Because . . . because . . . ," I stammered, unsure of how to explain myself.

"And that's real life too," she pressed on. "You're intruding on people's actual lives. But dreams aren't real. They're just silly stories, really."

"But I'm entering another person's mind!" I said, throwing my hands up.

"Do you not listen to me at all? You weren't in their minds. It's not like you could control them or anything. It's more like you're just participating in a story."

"This is so weird."

"It's just another element of your gift manifesting itself."

"But still. That story happens in their *head*. In their *brain*. What if my gift manifests itself in a new way and I can suddenly take control of someone's body or something?"

"Baylor," she said, frustrated. "How many times do I have to say it? You're not entering a person's mind."

I stared at her. "There's something you're not telling me."

She sighed. "It's complicated. It's not worth getting into."

"Tell me."

"Fine," she said impatiently. She stood up and closed her eyes, and a light dusting of blue energy began to emanate from her hand.

"What are you doing?" I asked.

"Sweet dreams, bro," she said, blowing the energy over me.

"What is——?"

But before I could finish speaking, I passed out and found myself in the star-filled dream room with Kristina.

"Where were we?" she asked.

"Well, we were chatting, and then you dream-drugged me," I said, amazed at how quickly I'd fallen asleep. "Pretty sure that's illegal in most states."

"We were talking about how you don't enter a person's mind when they're dreaming," she said, totally ignoring her crime. "In a nutshell, when people are asleep, their souls leave their bodies, and dreaming is what happens before and after the journey." She pointed down to the stars. "When these are illuminated, that means the person's dreaming and you can enter the dream, but when they're dim, the person's either awake or not available for visits."

"Wait," I said. "What? Their souls . . . they *what*?" She'd spoken as though she were teaching me some basic rule of life, like she was introducing gravity to me for the first time.

"See, this is why I didn't want to tell you," she said as the shooting stars that marked each door flickered at our feet. "It's complicated."

"Where do their souls go?"

"To learn lessons."

"But *where?*"

"In a place between here and the Beyond."

I rolled my eyes and took another look around. "And what is *here*, exactly? Where are we?"

She frowned. "It doesn't have a name, actually," she said, shrugging. "There's never really been a need to name it before you got here. The Dream Portal?"

I smiled smugly. Baylor Bosco, the grand adventurer, the brave explorer, the next great pioneer of the other side.

"Can you please wipe that dumb look off your face?" she asked.

"We can discuss names later, though I do think Baylorville has a nice ring to it," I said. "Anyway, isn't it dangerous for a soul to leave a body?"

"Nope," she said simply. "In fact, considering seven billion people do it every day, I'd say it's perfectly safe."

"But . . . but . . . that doesn't make sense," I said,

stammering to figure out exactly why it didn't make sense in my head. "How could a soul just leave a body? What if it got lost on the way back, and it ended up in the wrong place, and then two people wound up switching bodies?"

"That is," Kristina said, "quite possibly the dumbest question I've ever heard."

I frowned. It seemed perfectly reasonable to assume it could happen.

"But you should be aware of a few things."

"Okay," I said, my brain already feeling numb. There was so much I still had to learn about communicating with dead people, and now to have this new dream thing tacked on felt exhausting.

"It's rare, but demons can lurk here. Use caution, and always wear your amulet."

I shrugged. "Demons can lurk anywhere."

She nodded. "That brings me to my second point. Never trust someone who can't sleep," she said.

"What about Grandma Renee?" I asked. "She always stays up really late watching her soaps because she's got such a hard time sleeping."

"That's different," Kristina said. "Grandma's a saint."

"If she can't sleep, though . . . maybe she's hiding something."

"Allow me to rephrase," she said through gritted teeth. "When someone can't sleep, it can sometimes mean that something deep in their soul is desperately trying to keep them from sleeping."

"Because they don't want to go off and learn those lessons you talked about?"

She nodded. "Their soul resists it. They don't want to face what awaits them once they've drifted off."

"Because they get punished or something?"

"The truth is a tough thing to face sometimes," she said cryptically.

"But everyone has to sleep at some point," I said. "You'll die if you don't."

"They can get by on a few hours of restless sleep every night," Kristina said. "It's the dreamless parts—those blocks of time no one remembers once they've woken up—that matter. If you can't remember your dreams when you wake up, you've been off learning a *lot* of lessons." She jumped. "Speaking of which, I've got to head out to the Beyond. I'll see you in the morning. And remember, just because you can access other people's dreams doesn't mean you should."

I still had so many questions. What kind of lessons? And what point did they serve if I couldn't remember them when I woke up?

She gave me a pointed look and disappeared in

a zap of blue light before I could ask them. It's not like I was going to do anything weird. What was the worst that could happen? Still, her words bounced around in my mind as I strolled down the path to explore, and I decided not to dive into any dreams tonight. There were so many doors—I didn't count, but I couldn't believe how far the lane stretched on.

Once I'd reached the last door at the end of the path, I'd expected to hit some kind of wall, but instead, another incredible display of bright stars had appeared, somehow more incredible than what I'd just seen. Splashes of purple and blue colored the black canvas, space dust that drifted carelessly through the heavens. There were countless twinkling lights beckoning me forward to gaze into the infinite galaxies.

I stepped into the dancing lights and found myself transported seamlessly from the blackness of the Dream Portal to the blackness of an immense ocean, a light breeze blowing through my hair as the waves rolled gently by. The moon was nearly full and shining brightly, and together with the abundance of stars, they reflected off the surface of the ocean so vividly it was like I was swimming through the sky.

Was I back in my own dreams again? I didn't think so. I was still fully aware. I knew I was dreaming and not actually in the ocean. I didn't feel wet or cold. It was so peaceful.

Yet there was a sense of dread in the pit of my stomach, like no matter how serene and beautiful this setting was, something bigger was at play . . . something terrible.

I glanced around as a wave lifted me up and brought me back down. For a second, through the light of the moon and stars, I thought I saw a figure in the distance, but it disappeared. I stared hard, squinting, hoping my eyes would adjust and spot it again, but nothing happened.

I let the ocean wash over me for a while longer, but I couldn't relax. Soon enough, I wished I were actually dreaming and not partaking in this lucid dream.

If this were a real dream, then I could write off the feeling in my stomach as nothing more than the product of my overactive imagination.

If this were a real dream, I could wake up and laugh off the anxious feeling, not a care in the world.

But that wasn't the case. I was in someone else's dream, and the inexplicable dread and fear I felt were entirely too real.

TIP

6

Avoid your grandma's dreams.

THE NEXT MORNING I WENT FOR A BRISK bike ride around town to ward off the uneasy feeling gnawing at my stomach. Kristina kept asking me what was wrong, but I didn't want to make a big deal out of it. I was still new to this whole dreamwalking thing and just need to get a better grip on it.

First I visited Reverend Henry, who'd been a key part of helping me figure out the Sheet Man mystery. He'd just finished up a service, though, and I couldn't chat with him for too long since people had turned up in droves in anticipation of Thanksgiving.

An elderly woman in front of me was making persistent attempts to find a time to host him and his family for dinner soon, but he gracefully dodged every date she threw out. Behind me, the line of people was swarming with impatience.

"We'll find a time soon, Marietta," he said, pushing her away graciously but firmly. "Maybe after the holidays."

She left in a slow huff, and he turned back to me, his smile frozen in place.

He leaned forward and whispered, "Last time she had us over for dinner, we got stuck there for five hours. She warmed up a few cans of soup and showed us pictures of seventy years' worth of cats. My kids still haven't forgiven me."

I wanted to chat with him about my dreams, but the woman behind me stamped her foot rudely and glared at me when I turned to look at her.

"You didn't even attend the service," she said. "I saw you lock up your bike and get in line."

"Busted," I said, turning back to the reverend. "I'll see you later. Have a good Thanksgiving."

He winked at me as I turned to head back to my bike. "Ms. Holly," he said dryly to the woman behind me, "always such a joy to chat with someone so pleasant."

Then I headed to Madame Nadirah's Mystic Shoppe, but it was closed.

"What is this place?" Kristina asked as I walked over to read the handwritten sign on the door.

"Madame Nadirah was the one who helped me cross into the Sheet Man's weird dimension to find you, but then Grandpa came over and threw me out of it."

"Oh," Kristina said with a grimace. *"Her."*

I read the note on her door and chuckled.

Out sick today. If you need any merchandise, I'll be in tomorrow. If you need some spiritual healing, light a candle, pray you'll survive the night, and call me in the morning if you do. If it's an emergency, what's wrong with you?! Call 911!

Back at home I tried to help Mom prep some dishes for Thanksgiving, which was four days away, but I was distracted by what was to come that night. I couldn't wait to dream.

As I got ready for bed, I kept touching the amulet—a feeling of giddiness at the thought of hopping into other people dreams overshadowed the dread I'd felt earlier. I'd stick with the stars and avoid the creepy ocean that made my stomach queasy.

"You know," Kristina said delicately as I turned

off the lights, "just because you can go snooping through dreams doesn't mean you should."

She must have sensed my excitement.

"I'm not planning on making it a routine or anything. I'm just curious to see what else I can do, especially since you said it's so safe and all."

She hesitated for a moment. "I know I said it was safe, and it *is* safe, don't get me wrong. But it's safe for regular people. You're not a regular person, Baylor. I'm not saying anything's going to happen to you, but just . . . be careful."

I nodded. "I know, Kristina. I will."

I understood her caution. She was sort of responsible for me, after all, and lately keeping tabs on my safety seemed to become more difficult with each passing week.

That night, I dreamed I was back in homeroom. Aiden was trying to talk to J and failing spectacularly, so he started dancing for her right in the middle of the classroom. The scene seamlessly morphed into a rock concert, Aiden swaying silently onstage while the crowd rocked out before us, arms outstretched, heads banging, feet stomping.

I surveyed the scene, and the switch in my brain flipped.

This was a dream.

It wasn't real.

I brushed past the twirling Aiden and headed for the trapdoor in center of the stage.

"None of this is real," I announced to the crowd, but no one cared. Everyone was entranced with Aiden's pirouettes.

"Let's go," I said to no one, and the trapdoor descended into blackness. I stood back in my little dream universe, the shooting stars stretching left and right before me.

Something about this portal took me back to a water park I'd visited once when I was much younger. There'd been a ride called Starry Night where you went down a pitch-black tunnel on an inner tube by yourself, and as you sailed down, a bright, twinkling series of lights accompanied you the whole way. It had felt like soaring through space and seeing different galaxies.

This new Dream Portal was my own personal Starry Night, except it was much less wet (and likely much more sanitary). I still liked Baylorville as an option, but I decided to save it for a place that was accessible to more people than just Kristina and me.

I stepped past my own blue shooting star and turned right down the path. Was there any sort of rhyme or reason here as to which door belonged to whom? Could I get these labeled somehow, perhaps with some sort of dream label maker? I looked at my hand and imagined a label maker popping into being, but nothing happened.

Rats. I'd have to figure something else out to keep track of the doors.

I chose the one next to Ella's, figuring it was as good as any. I'd just have to come back night after night and explore the doors.

I tumbled forward into the darkness, somersaulting gracefully, but something weird happened. It felt like floating in a thick, jellylike haze, the surroundings partly visible through the gray. An unnaturally loud voice bellowed in my ears.

"Just $9.99 if you call now! Our EZ-Omelet makes the perfect gift for any occasion! And if you call in the next five minutes, we'll throw in a free gift—the Perfect Pancake Molder!"

Who on earth was dreaming of an infomercial? I squinted through the haze and could barely make out a TV. Then a man entered into view—he turned off the TV, and the blaring voice went away. Then he walked over in my direction, and I gasped. It was Grandpa By! He was rapidly fading away, and I wasn't sure it was really him since he was wearing an oversize chef's hat and juggling pancakes. Was she imagining this whole scenario?

"Sleep tight, my sweet, lovely Renee," he whispered, blowing kisses in my direction. "You are my world and my wonder." Then he disappeared, along with the haze, and for a second I was shrouded in total darkness before I reemerged into some sort of playground teeming with kids. It looked really old-fashioned, mainly because of the outfits. Lots of plaid, high socks, clunky shoes, and huge glasses, like they'd robbed a museum of 1960s fashion

"You coming, Renee?" A group of girls giggled. I turned to my left and saw my grandma Renee as a teenager. I recognized her from all the photo albums I've looked through at her house. She had these bright blue eyes, wide and deerlike. They reminded me of Kristina's.

"Ugh, fine," Grandma said with a shrug, looking my way. "You coming, B.?"

I widened my eyes. How did she know who I was? I wasn't even close to being alive at this point in history! But then I remembered this dream was happening right now, in real time. Obviously if I traveled back in time, teenager Renee wouldn't know me, but in this weird dream world, Grandma Renee did.

"Sure," I said. "Where are we going?"

She jerked her head to the left, and I followed her gaze to two girls sitting on some bleachers. One was almost supernaturally tall, to the point where her body shape was more ostrich than human, while the other was unnaturally rotund, as though she were part walrus. Surely Grandma's mind was misremembering them.

We walked in unison over to the girls, who didn't look pleased to see us.

"Hey, Fatty Patty and Legsy Lisa," Grandma said. I jerked my whole body her way.

"What did you say?" I asked, shocked, but she ignored me.

"Listen, you losers aren't planning on coming to my party this weekend, right?" she continued.

The shorter, rounder girl gulped. She seemed to grow more walruslike by the second, to the point where I was expecting tusks to burst from her face. "Isn't it a class party?"

"Right," Grandma said, "but you two aren't really part of the class, you know? You're just the two freaks we all sort of feel sorry for." She looked at her nails. "I wouldn't want you feeling left out when no one talks to you. Plus, you'd probably just gross all the boys out."

My insides had turned to ice, and I couldn't suppress my gasp. "Grandma!"

Grandma Renee looked at me in shock for a split

second, before the scene dissolved away into nothing. I felt a sudden lurch in the pit of my stomach, and with a soft *pop*, I found myself tumbling forcibly backward into the Starry Night.

I stood there, panting slightly. Grandma Renee had just bullied the daylights out of those girls. Was that what she was like when she was younger?

Her look of shock was imprinted onto my mind. In that brief moment, her face had transformed from the smooth and youthful one of her past to the wrinkled, soft one I knew so well. It was almost like she'd realized it was actually me, her grandson, witnessing her horrible behavior, and had come back to herself. She'd probably woken up right at the moment, which is why I was forced back into the Starry Night.

I wanted to wake myself up to call her and ask if the dream had been something real from her past, but I didn't think that would go over well. I hadn't yet told my parents about the dreamwalking, and if I called her, she'd certainly tell them all about it. Plus, I felt a bit weird. I'd entered her dream uninvited and witnessed something she was probably embarrassed about. The next time I saw her was going to be really awkward.

I looked down at her shooting star, but saw it was no longer illuminated. There was only a very faint gray glow marking the door. Weird. I guessed it meant she wasn't dreaming anymore, which only helped to confirm my theory she'd suddenly woken up.

I went to the door across from hers and hesitated a moment. After experiencing Grandma Renee's dream, did I really want to go through another one?

But then I thought back to Bobby's dream and how pleasant and interesting it had been. I couldn't stop just yet! Besides, how much worse could it get than discovering your loving grandma was once a mean girl?

Resolute, I took a step forward, tumbling and landing in a familiar hallway. I was in Aiden's house, though it looked much darker than usual, with long, creepy shadows looming over the walls.

The sound of a loud, angry voice reached my ears. I had never heard the voice in this house before, and I was suddenly very wary. I crept forward, cringing at a torrent of words spewing venomously from the mouth of an apparently furious woman, and peeked around the corner into the kitchen. The entire space had been cleared away of cabinets and appliances. Aiden was handcuffed to a chair, a single bulb lit over his head, like he was in a top secret interrogation room. Mrs. Kirkwood, who was normally so kind and friendly, was spewing abuse.

You never lift a finger in this—*my*—house. Why am I coming home to see this garbage can full? Too lazy to do anything around here? It's no wonder you're so fat, only watching TV all day like some worthless blob."

I crept into the kitchen hidden in the shadows, letting them cover me like an invisibility cloak.

She backed out of the room, and J took her place and glared at her boyfriend. "I'm only dating you because I feel sorry for you." Aiden recoiled, and she clearly took great pleasure in causing him pain. "Look at you. Who could ever like you? It's embarrassing. *You're* embarrassing."

She scoffed at him and then disappeared from the room. Someone else walked in, and I jumped with surprise to see me walking toward Aiden. Except it didn't quite look like me. I was a little taller, a little better looking.

"I can't wait to get to high school and leave you behind," I said, my voice as cold as a winter's night in Keene. "You're such a loser. You're lucky I pity you so much."

My heart was pounding inside of my chest, and I stepped forward out of the shadows.

"That's not true!" I said, touching his shoulder.

He winced horribly, like I'd hit him, then stared at

me in confusion from his wet eyes. He looked from the Baylor yelling at him to the Baylor consoling him several times.

I realized I shouldn't be there. I had to leave. Aiden wouldn't want me to see his deepest insecurities laid out so plainly. I lunged back down the shadowy hall-way, my heart threatening to burst from my chest, but before I could get back to the Starry Night I shot up awake in bed, breathing hard.

I'd been lucid dreaming, but really, I'd been in a nightmare. Aiden's nightmare.

I sat there trying to catch my breath. I knew I was going to be up for a while. How would I be able to fall back to sleep tonight after discovering that my best friend dreamed about his loved ones saying the most hateful things imaginable to him?

Nobody is worthless.

I HADN'T BEEN ABLE TO FALL BACK ASLEEP, and by the time Kristina reappeared around six o'clock in the morning. I was surrounded by candles, trying to cleanse my space of any negative vibes I may have picked up from Aiden's nightmare.

"What happened?" Kristina said, suspicious. "You're up far too early and surrounded by far too many candles for me to think everything is okay here."

I sighed. "I went exploring last night."

She stared at me hard and her mouth puckered. "Go on."

"Well, who should I begin with? Grandma or Aiden?"

"Grandma."

"In her dream, she was bullying some girls at school and being a total jerk. It was horrible."

She nodded, looking over my shoulders and out the window. "And Aiden?"

"His mom, J, and I all took turns shoving his insecurities down his throat. It was *also* horrible."

"Baylor, I don't want to sound like Mom, but what did I tell you about walking through dreams?"

"If you don't want to sound like Mom right now, you're doing a horrible job."

"You have a choice here. It's your mission in life to pass on healing messages, but you don't have to walk through dreams; honestly, it's very intrusive. You may as well just walk in the bathroom while Grandma's taking a shower and rip open the curtain!"

"What!" I shrieked, slapping my hands to cover my eyes. "Why would you say that? That's in no way the same thing!"

"Secondly," she continued, unfazed, "it's going to affect your opinion of people. You don't know that any of these things actually happened in real life. Maybe Grandma was reliving some bad experience from her past, or maybe it was, you know, a *dream*."

"It seemed like more than a dream to me," I said, still trying to burn away images from my eyeballs. "And Aiden's was definitely real. Well, the feelings behind it, I mean."

"My point is, you don't know the extent of the reality here, and you're never going to know because, to even ask the question, you'd have to admit that you spied on their dreams and invaded their privacy."

"Or," I said, brainstorming out loud, "I could strongly hint at certain things around them and see how they react?"

"Oh, yeah, great idea," Kristina said sarcastically. "So what's the plan for Aiden? You're just going to casually hint around about what a loser he is?"

"Well, I haven't really figured that part out yet, Kristina," I said. "I'll get there."

"Don't be a jerk about it," she said tensely. "The last thing Aiden needs is for his friend to act so nosy and insensitive about something he's clearly sensitive about."

"I am *offended* you'd even suggest such a thing," I said, feeling surprised and a bit proud at how protective she'd sounded of him.

"Good," she said with a vindictive look in her eye. "It's about time I offended you as much as your tuba's offended my ears the last couple weeks. I'll never get over that mash-up."

"That's a bit rude. It didn't sound *that* bad."

"Baylor, Beethoven could hear it in the Beyond, and he was weeping like a little girl."

In homeroom later that morning, Aiden looked frazzled.

"What's up with you?" I asked, a bit hesitantly.

"Nothing, nothing," he said too quickly. "Just pretty tired. Ready for Thanksgiving break to start." We only had to get through today and tomorrow before break began on Wednesday.

"Tired?" I asked, lasering in. "Did you not sleep well?"

He side-eyed me and said cryptically, "I've slept better."

"Oh? Why? Bad dream?"

"Snoyes," he stammered in one jumbled mess.

"What?"

"Nothing," he said, glancing around the room. "I mean, sort of."

I held my breath, hoping he'd discuss the dream with me.

"I dreamed," he said, pausing for a split second, "that Mr. G. kept yelling at me and telling me how worthless I am." He swallowed hard.

"Oh," I said, feeling my stomach turn to ice as a

storm of sadness crossed his face. He pressed his lips together so his cheeks grew wider, like a devastated chipmunk.

"That's really . . . rough," I said.

He nodded.

"You know you're not, though. Right, Aiden?" I said, chills suddenly pulsing through my body. "Don't think about it for even one more second because that's so wrong, and to entertain the possibility that what your m—uh, what Mr. G. said could remotely be true is one of the dumbest things you could ever do."

Aiden looked at me, his eyes scrunched in confusion. "What are you talking about, Baylor?"

"Nothing," I said quickly. "I . . . I just wanted to remind you it was only a dream."

Suspicion crossed his face, but he looked away.

There's no way he can know you were actually in his dream. No way. How could he possibly figure that one out?

But there was that one second, right before I left, when Aiden had winced as he looked at me, and I got the sudden feeling I shouldn't be there. I wondered how many times he'd had that dream; my bet was it happened pretty often, but that was probably the first time a second Baylor had showed up to comfort him.

But still, my presence didn't immediately prove to him that I was actually in his dream. If anything, it just further confirmed that he was having an insane dream. As far as he was concerned, my presence was merely an extension of his subconscious, something for him to root out and decipher on his own time.

That night I got into bed, quickly fell asleep, battled a merciless talking fish and his urchin army, realized I was dreaming, and then found myself back in the Starry Night.

But I was hesitant to move forward. If I entered anyone else's dreams, what was I going to find? More character assassinations like in Grandma Renee's dream? More deep-rooted insecurities like in Aiden's dream? I thought of my mom and her habit of chopping things when she's nervous; what if in her dreams she didn't limit it to just vegetables, but took glee in stabbing anything that crossed her path?

It was enough to make me want to go hang out with Bobby and Mr. Moose. I bet Ella dreamed in fun ways, too, with talking dolphins and life-size Barbies whirling about. Why couldn't everyone's dreams be so simple?

It was no use. I wouldn't be able to visit anyone tonight. I'd just have to try—

All of sudden, a bright flash of light erupted over the Starry Night like a dangerous lightning storm, followed by a cataclysmic *bang*, the force shaking my face and borderline rupturing my eardrums. I looked up and discovered a horrible face staring back at me.

TIP
8

Loved Ones is a very, uh, loose phrase.

DISORIENTED FROM THE FLASH OF LIGHT and the ringing in my ears, I lunged backward, trying to fling myself away from the spirit, but I must have stepped away from my shooting star during the chaos because I was still in the Starry Night.

"Really, kid? You're still that mad at me?"

I untangled myself and stood up to find an old woman staring down at me in amusement. She looked familiar . . . actually, she *sounded* familiar, her voice deep and gravelly, like sandpaper had withered away her vocal cords.

"How do I know you?" I asked.

A rough laugh croaked out of her. "Aw, come on, kid, it's only been a few weeks!"

I didn't appreciate her tone. It had been an eventful few weeks, and I'd come across a ton of spirits. But there was something so distinct about her voice that it unlocked a memory in my brain.

"You're Aunt Hilda's friend," I said slowly. "Marjorie!"

Earlier this month, my aunt Hilda had celebrated her eighty-eighth birthday at an Italian restaurant, and it was a disaster. For some unknown reason, Kristina and I can't tune out spirits in Italian restaurants, and I wound up causing a scene and ruining her birthday.

Afterward my parents forced me to go to her apartment and apologize in person. Except when I got there, I ended up delivering a message from Marge, who'd just crossed over the night before, and Aunt Hilda didn't know her friend had died. It was not a great situation.

"Good news," she said, throwing her hands up. "My cats didn't eat my body!"

I grimaced. "That's . . . great."

"You're telling me. I just wish I'd asked you to erase my Internet browser history. My daughters . . . oh boy, did they get a shock."

"Marge, can I help you with something?" I said quickly, slapping my hands to my eyes, hoping she would go away, or at the very least stop talking. "What are you even doing here?"

"I'm visiting Hilda, of course," she said. "I like to check in on her."

"You're what?"

She frowned at me. "You new to this, kid?"

"Well, I'm not exactly an expert yet, considering the fact that I'm still, you know, alive and everything."

"Show off," she grumbled, crossing her arms across her chest. "Well, we not-alive people can visit alive people in their dreams."

"What? But isn't this my Dream Portal? Why would you have to go through me to visit Aunt Hilda?"

"Oh, I'm sorry, your majesty!" she said in mock concern. She snorted unpleasantly. "Do you think you own Loved Ones' Lane?"

"Loved Ones' Lane? Is that"—I motioned to the blackness and the shooting stars all around us— "what you call this? I've been calling it the Starry Night."

"The Starry Night? Original. I'll let van Gogh know about your tribute when I run into him. I call it Loved Ones' Lane as an homage to my checkered past." She giggled at a passing memory that I had no desire to hear about. "This is the entryway to our loved ones' dreams."

"What? So all ghosts use this lane to enter dreams?" Kristina had neglected to mention that tidbit.

"Pretty much," she said. Her voice was so cacophonous that she may as well have been gurgling rocks. "It's not like I can visit just anyone, though. I can't drop in on the president and give him an earful on his antismoking initiative, as much as I'd like to. The lane is personalized to each ghost. And you and I happen to have Hilda in common, kid."

"So you can't drop in on my baby sister?" I pointed to the door across from me.

"Sure can't," she said, looking at the door. "That's the entryway for my grandson." She sighed. "I probably don't have nearly as many doors as you do. You're young. You've got a lot of living people around— friends, cousins, siblings. I've got, what? Maybe ten doors left."

I looked down my lane and smiled. It was pretty long.

Marjorie looked down at Aunt Hilda's shooting star; it was getting noticeably dimmer.

"Sorry, kid, wish I could stay and chat more, but she's about to head off," Marge said. "Gotta go." She took a step forward, but before she tumbled away, she looked at me once more. "You should really visit her more, kid. She's an old lady and doesn't have many friends left. She'd be glad to see you."

Before I could argue and say that Aunt Hilda would actually hate to see more of me, she somersaulted through the door and disappeared.

A part of me wanted to follow her through the door. What would happen if two souls suddenly infiltrated Aunt Hilda's dream? Maybe she'd start getting nicer! I could sneak in every night and slowly hypnotize her into accepting my gift.

You love Baylor's gift.

Baylor is your favorite.

Send Baylor ten dollars every week.

I doubted Kristina would approve of that sort of subterfuge, but how would she ever find out? Maybe she'd get suspicious if she noticed Aunt Hilda suddenly treating me better. She couldn't prove anything, though, and if the plan worked and Aunt Hilda and I became pals, then, really, what would be the problem?

I made a mental note to try that out in the future. I still needed to explore the Starry N—uh, Loved Ones' Lane before committing to that kind of action; plus, I really didn't want to have to keep dealing with Marge.

I decided to walk down the lane and see how many

doors I could count. As far as I could tell, there was no way to distinguish between them. I wondered how Marge knew which one was which. Maybe it was different for ghosts. It was possible her time spent in the Beyond, however short it had been thus far, had already prepared her on how to navigate the lane. In a way, that made sense—the lane was meant for ghosts, not for curious thirteen-year-old mediums.

I counted fifty-seven doors down the lane before the shooting stars disappeared, and I was struck by a wave of confusion. Assuming my door was in the middle of the lane, I could easily have access to 114 people. And not just people, but *loved ones*, as both Kristina and Marge had said.

I didn't have 114 loved ones. No way. I thought I'd max out at forty, tops.

Off the top of my head, I could only count my immediate family, my three living grandparents, Aunt Hilda, Aiden, J, Bobby, Reverend Henry, and probably Aiden's mom, too. Then a bunch of aunts and uncles and cousins, so that brought the number to just over forty.

I'm not sure who on the other side decided on the definition of "loved ones," but they needed to dial it down a notch. The shooting star in front of the last door on the lane shimmered brightly, and curiosity got the better of me. I needed to find out who had barely made the cut.

I tumbled through the door, somersaulted forward, and drifted down into a large lecture hall, where all the students were furiously taking notes as the professor rambled on about bloodstain patterns. Everyone seemed much older than me, so I guessed it was a college course. Then I noticed most of the students weren't using pens to take notes. They were using their bloody fingers to jot down the professor's words about spatter and arterial spray.

"I'm so pleased to have such a dedicated group of students," the professor purred, observing his class with a disturbing hunger in his eyes. The only thing missing from his evil professor look was a bald, wrinkled cat for him to lightly stroke. "Extra credit to all those who bled for their education today."

Students were pale and groaning in pain as the blood dripped out of them. The guy sitting in front of me brushed his hand through his hair, leaving a streak of bright red, and as the hair settled back into place, the blood flicked off and landed on my face.

It was time to go.

"Gross," said a voice to my right. I knew it instantly. I'd gotten into major trouble a few weeks back just to hear that voice for a few minutes.

Will Parker, son of the Sheet Man, wiped away blood from his left cheek and swatted it from his hand toward the ground.

"I hate this class," he muttered.

He was getting his masters in criminology in Boston, and it didn't take long to piece together that he was stressed out about one of his forensics classes.

"Everything all right, Will?"

He turned toward me and frowned.

"I didn't know you were in this class, Baylor."

"Yeah," I said. "I'm definitely going to drop it, though. It's a little bloodier than I'm used to."

He nodded. "This guy's a pyscho."

"Any idea how I can get out of here?"

"Go out the door," he said. "Obviously."

"Right," I said, standing up, "I'll see you later."

"Come to my study group later so we can prep for finals."

"Will do," I said, heading up the aisle toward the exit. I pushed through the doors and tumbled back to Loved Ones' Lane.

Will Parker? Really? He counted as a loved one? That seemed like a real stretch to me. I liked the guy just fine, but I hardly knew him. I guess I did feel a bizarre kinship with him since his father haunted me for a few weeks and kidnapped Kristina, all thanks to his mother. Not to mention the fact that his mother was suddenly taken away to God-knows-where by a Bruton. I doubted we'd ever see her again. He and his sister didn't get a chance to say good-bye, which was sort of sad, even if she was a lunatic who tried to murder me.

I wanted to keep exploring the fringes of my loved ones, but just past Will's door the ocean and brilliant night sky had appeared again. I squinted hard, wondering if anything was out there, when I suddenly spotted it—a weird misshapen figure, like one of Jack's bad LEGO creations, just barely reflecting the moonlight.

I hopped off the edge of the lane, swan-diving down through the air and into the ocean, heading straight for it.

The figure transformed before my eyes as I got closer. There was a big horizontal part, slightly curved and shiny white, and on either side of it were two more shapes, but I couldn't tell what they were.

After a few more minutes I got to the shape and discovered the curved horizontal piece had that white, shiny gloss that has made up the surface of every boat I've ever seen. Except this one was capsized, and lying on top of it were two kids, both about my age. One was a dark-skinned boy, the other was a girl with a mane of wavy brunette hair, and both looked like they'd been through hell. Their skin—hers a deep olive, his as black as the shadowy ocean—was burned and mottled, their lips dry and cracked. Their clothes were tattered, wet, and sticking to their skin.

Who were they? Was this real? Was I in a dream?

"Hello?" I said gently. "Can you hear me?"

The boy slowly cracked open an eye and stared at me.

"I'm starting to hallucinate, Helena," he said, his voice surprisingly deep. He clutched a half-full water bottle that was strapped around his wrist. "There's a kid floating in the ocean." The girl didn't respond.

"Who are you?" I asked.

"Me? You're the one in my dream. Who are you?"

"My name's Baylor," I said. "So, this is a dream then?"

"It could be," he said. "But it might not be. All I can remember anymore is the water. It's everywhere, all the time; when I'm awake, when I'm asleep. It's all I know now."

"But why?"

"Because we made a mistake," he said. "And now, it's too—"

But he didn't finish. A huge wave smacked into us,

and before I knew it, I'd zoomed back to Loved Ones' Lane and saw that the giant ocean had evaporated.

Tuesday passed by in a mix of euphoria and discontent. It was the last day before Thanksgiving break, and none of the teachers were even bothering to try. In fact, before I left home that morning, Dad was humming merrily as he fiddled with the coffeemaker.

"It's one of the best days of the year, Baylor," he said with a grin as he snuggled with his mug of coffee, clasping it between his hands and holding it just below his chin. He breathed in deeply and sighed.

"Why's that?" I asked, totally drained from the dreamwalking. I couldn't get the image of those two kids out of my head. Had that been real? I needed to talk to Kristina about it, but I wanted to discuss it in depth and wouldn't have time for that until later.

"Because I get to play games with my students all day, and then it's a five-day weekend." He chuckled. "I love the holidays."

He worked at the high school, but all the teachers at the middle school got the memo, too. English class turned into an open reading period, and during social studies we watched battered VCR recordings of classic news segments.

It was clear the day was a joke, and by lunchtime I

was wondering if I could escape the premises and slip home unnoticed. As I was plotting out a strategy in the lunch line—today was the Thanksgiving special, complete with slimy turkey slices, cold corn, and mashed potatoes that tasted like recycled cardboard—someone grabbed my shoulder and yanked me out of line.

"What'd you do to my brother, Bosco?" asked Cam Nguyen, his sizable cheeks looking rosier than usual after he'd dragged me a few feet away where no one could hear us. Cam was in the grade below me and also in the band, and I instantly remembered the incident on Saturday. It was his little brother I'd accidentally scared.

"Oh, listen Cam, I'm sorry if I scared him," I said. "I thought he and his friends were bullying Jack, but it was all a misunderstanding."

"Minh's not a bully," he said, still furious. "If anyone's a bully here, it's you. He hasn't slept for the last few nights because you scared him so bad."

"Scared him? But . . . but I didn't scare him," I said. "I just talked to him."

"He said you were talking to a ghost," he hissed, lowering his voice as he said the word "ghost."

"His grandpa," Kristina said, flittering over. "You never actually delivered that message because all the kids ran away scared."

"That's true," I said, nodding. "It was actually your grandpa, now that I'm, uh, thinking of it. He said to tell you—well, actually Minh, but I'm sure you're a good alternative—that he misses you."

Cam's eyes turned dark. "This . . . this is the problem! You go around thinking everyone wants to hear stuff like that, Baylor, but not everyone does," he said, throwing his hands up. "Especially not a seven-year-old who's still afraid of the dark. He used to get by with three night-lights, but lately we've had to leave all his lights on just so he doesn't feel scared in his room."

"Is there a problem here, gentlemen?" asked Mr. Connell, the toad-voiced vice-principal. He scuttled over from the end of the line and gave us each a once-over. "You're not going to make the last day before break a difficult one for me, are you?"

"No, sir," Cam said, though he was still glaring at me. "I was just leaving."

"That's what I thought," he said as Cam walked to his table, crushing his brown paper lunch bag in his fist. "Baylor Bosco, I don't know what's gotten into you this year, but trouble seems to have taken a liking to you."

I shrugged. "It's my calling, I guess."

Sharks aren't the scariest things the ocean has to offer.

EVERYONE CHEERED AFTER THE FINAL BELL rang. On our walk out, Bobby was bouncing in excitement.

"No school for five days," he said dreamily. "I feel like singing! *Five-day weekend, five-day weekend, just for me, just for me. Then I get to eat a ton, turkey, turkey, turkey, turkey, just for me, just for me.*"

Aiden, J, and I gawked at him as he kept humming the tune of his own special song. Kristina hovered just over his shoulder as if she were trying to check inside his ears.

"He must have a fever," she muttered to herself.

"Bobby," J said sharply, "if you ever do that again, our friendship is over."

"Please, J," he said, smiling widely. "You'd last four minutes before you'd come crawling back to me."

J suppressed a smile and shook her head. "I think I'd be just fine, thank you very much."

"Who'd be fine in a world without Bobby Wackendorf?" he asked in horror. "I shudder at the thought of it."

Aiden was taking in the conversation in his usual awkward way, perpetually flustered that anyone could talk to J without first having to count to ten and take several deep breaths. He'd never admitted it to me, but I knew he was jealous of Bobby's sheer effortlessness when it came to talking. I could almost see Aiden studying Bobby whenever he spoke, mentally taking notes on how to act cool. Then I pictured him trying to be cool in front of the mirror in his bathroom at home, and I shook my head. I really hoped that wasn't true.

"Everyone's staying in town for break, right?" asked J. "Let's hang out on Friday or Saturday."

"My cousins are going to be in town for Thanksgiving," I said, "but as long as they can come?"

"The more the merrier!" J said to me. She turned to Bobby and Aiden. "Do you guys have any visitors?"

"Lots of cousins," Bobby said, "but they're all either ten years older or ten years younger than me, so I won't be inviting them to come hang out with us, unless you guys want to spend two hours at Build-A-Bear."

Aiden's eyes flashed in excitement, and I frowned at him.

"I'm sure he'd love another for his collection," Kristina said to me, smirking.

"What about you, Aiden?" J asked.

"Um . . . it's just me and my mom this year," he said, looking at his shoes. "Usually my grandparents come in, but they couldn't make it."

"Oh," J said. She turned to me and her eyebrows shot up. I shrugged. "That's a bummer."

"It's fine," he said quickly, scanning the cars in the pick-up lane. "We'll probably just get some pizza since it's a lot for my mom to cook for just two people. Oh, there she is." Through the front passenger window we could see Mrs. Kirkwood leaning over the center console and waving at us with both hands. "Text me about the plans. And happy Thanksgiving!" He smiled weakly and scrambled to the car. We could just make out Mrs. Kirkwood screaming "Hi, kids!" before Aiden slammed the door shut.

As they drove away, J looked at me and frowned.

"I feel terrible. It's just the two of them for Thanksgiving dinner? And they're going to order a pizza?"

"Depressing," Bobby said, shaking his head.

"I didn't know, either," I said.

"I'm sure Mom wouldn't mind having them over," Kristina said.

I nodded. "Maybe they can come to the Bosco Thanksgiving extravaganza?"

"You should ask your mom!" J said as she waved to her dad. "I gotta go, but let me know how it goes."

Thanksgiving was my mom's time to shine. Chopping random vegetables in the kitchen was her main form of stress relief, and figuring out how to combine them in creative, not disgusting ways had become a specialty of hers. Through the years, she learned you can mix just about anything into a casserole and no one will really know the difference as long as there's enough cheese in it.

After I was home, I told Mom what Aiden had said. She looked horrified.

"Oh no," she said, tears welling up in her eyes. "I feel awful."

"Well, it's not too late to invite them over, right?" I shrugged, eating one of the cookies she'd baked to celebrate the long break. "Just call her."

"That's not it," she said, putting her hand over her

face. "I was telling Karen last week how I was so happy it was going to be *just family* this year, with none of the random stragglers we've had over the last couple years."

It was true—our Thanksgivings usually turned into a Who's Who of misfits. Last year Grandma Renee had invited a few people from her church who had nowhere else to go, and the year before that Aunt Hilda had invited two of her friends who'd then invited a couple of their friends without telling her. Before we knew it, we'd had eight extra people at the house, and my dad had to run to the store to buy rotisserie chickens so they could trick people into thinking they had enough food.

"I don't understand the problem," I said. "She won't remember you saying that. I can text Aiden if you don't want to tell Mrs. Kirkwood."

"Of course she'll remember I said that," she said, incredulous. "I was such a jerk about it. I went on and on about how it was going to be enjoyable this year without having to worry about any of the charity cases that have been showing up." She groaned. "It was not my finest moment."

"She's not going to think she's a charity case," I said.

"Baylor, you are so sweet and innocent and naive,"

she said, kissing the top of my head. "That's exactly what she's going to think."

Kristina chuckled. "Silly Baylor," she said. "So naive."

I called J afterward to tell her what my mom said.

"I don't get the problem," I said. "I'll just text Aiden and tell him to come. I really don't think his mom would remember."

"Baylor, how dumb are you?" J said. "Of course Mrs. Kirkwood's going to remember. I *guarantee* you that if you invited them over now, she'd only feel like a charity case. She'd come up with some excuse as to why she and Aiden wouldn't be able to join." She sighed. "Your poor mom. I bet she feels awful."

"Women are so weird," I said. "You think too much."

"Maybe you don't think enough," J snapped.

Kristina laughed from the bed and said, "She's got that right."

I glared at her as J kept speaking. "Even if we can't save his Thanksgiving, maybe there's something else we can do to help him. He needs a confidence boost. I mean, he's too scared to even hold my hand!"

"What do you have in mind?" I asked.

"I'm not sure yet," she said slowly, clearly tossing around a million ideas in her mind. "But I'll think of something."

After I hung up the phone, Kristina was smiling

dreamily. "I like J. She keeps you on your toes."

"You just like her because she snaps at me like you do. You see too much of yourself in her."

"Only the good qualities," she said. "Nothing wrong with that."

"We have very different definitions of *good*," I said.

"Yes," she said. "And mine's the better one."

"Anyway," I said, eager to change the subject, "I'm just happy break is starting. I need a few days to process this whole dreamwalking thing. It's starting to really mess with me."

She frowned. "What happened now? Why didn't you say anything earlier?"

"Too tired," I said. "I feel like I haven't gotten any sleep."

"Well, maybe if you would just stay put in your own dreams for a while, there wouldn't be a problem," she said irritably.

"But there's too much to explore," I said, rubbing my eyes. Then I remembered my revelatory little chat with Marge. "I ran into Aunt Hilda's friend Marge. You don't know her because Rosalie had already nabbed you at that point, but last night she told me about the Dream Portal. She calls it Loved Ones' Lane. You failed to mention that ghosts could use the same room to visit people too."

She turned away, fidgeting with something on her ghost shirt. "Did I?" she mumbled.

"You sure did," I said. "Why didn't you tell me? Do you ever visit Mom and Dad?"

She nodded, still going to town at the invisible thread on her shirt.

"How often?"

She straightened her already pristine skirt. "Fairly regularly."

"Wait a second. That means they can see you, though."

"When they see me, they think I'm Ella as a teenager," she said quietly. "And I don't bother to correct them."

"But why?" I asked. "You could have had a relationship with them all this time."

"It doesn't work that way, Baylor," she said sadly. "Ghosts can't just drop in whenever they want. The visits are reserved for special circumstances, and they're meant to pass on comforting messages and vibes from the Beyond. I can't just start a relationship with them in their dreams."

"Why not? That's exactly what you can do."

"Maybe in a lucid dream," she said, "but in a regular dream it just wouldn't work. They're too outlandish. I'd be asking Mom to pay attention to me while she's running around in a cooking competition, trying to cut her vegetables with dull spoons or something." She shrugged, her face wistful. "I just like to be with them sometimes."

"That's so depressing," I said. "Does Mom really dream about stuff like that?"

She nodded. "She's a Food Network Star in her dreams."

"I'll have to check out her show one of these nights," I said, laughing. "Can you explain something, though? Why would Will Parker show up as one of my loved ones? That makes no sense to me."

"You forged a strong bond with him and Isabella, even if you don't realize it now," she said.

"But I wouldn't say they were my loved ones," I said.

She shrugged. "It's not up to you."

"What?"

"That's decided in the Beyond."

"That doesn't seem fair," I said. "I should have a say over who shows up in my lane."

"Well, sorry, Baylor, but that's just the way it is. It's never been an issue before since the Beyond never had to account for bratty teenage mediums."

"I will consider your apology," I said. "Though, to be frank, it didn't sound that sincere."

"Gosh, you're smart," she said sarcastically.

"I have another question about the dreams," I said. It felt like a scratchy rope with a ten-pound weight was tied around my vocal cords.

"You've got to be kidding. Let it go."

"Just listen. At the end of my lane I keep seeing this ocean scene. It doesn't seem like a dream, though. It looks just like a real night sky and a big wavy sea. I thought I saw something in the distance, but I couldn't be sure. At first it felt like something was really wrong, but the second time it happened, I swam out and talked to this kid. He was with a girl, and they were on an overturned boat. I talked to him for a second, but then a wave hit and I was right back on the lane."

Kristina looked at me like I had grown an extra ear in the middle of my forehead. "You didn't go through a dream door?" she asked, her voice tense.

"Nope," I said. "It sort of just happened."

"That's . . . bizarre. Believe me, there's no beach access off Loved Ones' Lane for any of the other ghosts who use it. Ghosts hate the ocean."

"What do you mean?"

"The ocean's just a big void to ghosts because there's no people in it," she said. "It's a vast empty space, and they're afraid of getting sucked out to sea and lost forever."

"Lost forever? Can't they just cross back into the Beyond?"

"It's not that easy. Living people serve as the focal points for ghosts. If ghosts get separated from loved ones, there's no easy way for them to return to the Beyond, and they're endangering the welfare of their eternal souls." She shook her head. "They're called the Lost Souls. Sometimes they find their way back, but a lot more of them wind up wandering for years, and before long, they transform."

"Into what?"

"It depends. Sometimes they just disappear and become part of the Earth's energy. Sometimes they devolve into demons. I've heard the Bermuda Triangle's swarming with Ashens and who knows what else."

Ashens are new, freshly converted demons. They're the least dangerous of all the demons, which is the equivalent of saying rat poison is the least poisonous of all the poisons. They're still bad, but there are much, much worse.

She frowned. "The Lost Souls are so far gone that they've become devoted to evil and deception. Tricking boat crews and airplane pilots, wreaking havoc, and feasting upon the souls of innocent people caught in their wake of destruction and death. They have no choice but to drift along with them forever, and soon enough, they transform too."

"Are you kidding me?" I said. "They sound like an evil motorcycle gang of the seas."

"Kind of. The ocean is a mysterious force," she said with a shrug. "I mean, why do you think people like going to the beach so much?"

"Because people find the ocean relaxing?"

"Exactly. Most people don't go to the beach to roll around in the sand. They're there for the ocean, even if they don't realize it. Spirits steer clear of the ocean to avoid the Lost Souls, and that makes it easier for people to relax."

"Well, it's also beautiful and fun," I said.

"Right," Kristina said, nodding, "because the spirits aren't there to bother them."

"I feel like it would still be relaxing and beautiful and fun even if the spirits were brave enough to show up."

"That's unlikely."

"I'm pretty sure it's very likely."

"I guess we'll never know," she said brightly.

"Right. So if I'm randomly dreaming of oceans, does that mean my soul could get sucked away too?"

"You're not a ghost," she said. "You're fine."

"But then what could it be? Whose dream was it?"

She hesitated. "It could be any number of reasons, Baylor. Hopefully it won't happen again." Except that it had already happened a couple times, and there was no reason for it to not occur again. That sense of dread I'd felt was too real for me to ignore, and I couldn't help but suspect someone—or some spirit—might have needed my help.

That night, though, after I watched Mom beat Bobby Flay in a grilling competition, I walked to the end of the lane and found the stars and the moon and the oceans waiting for me. I searched through the vast, dimly lit expanse for some clue, for a dark figure in the shadows, and I jumped off the edge of the lane and propelled myself in the direction I'd gone before. As I got closer, though, another shape popped up and distracted me.

It was a very faint, thin band of white in the shape of a rectangle, far out in the distance, hovering in the sky. I changed directions and headed for the rectangle. As I swam, the amulet warmed against my chest, but my attention quickly turned back to the strange shape. No matter how hard I swam toward it, though, it stayed the same distance away from me, completely out of reach.

10

Cleaning is still worse than any nightmare.

"RISE AND SHINE, MY DEAR FAMILY," MOM called from downstairs. The unmistakable scent of bacon wafted into my nose, and I immediately hopped out of bed and ran downstairs.

"Bacon?" I asked Mom, and she smiled and pointed to the kitchen table.

"And eggs, and pancakes," she said. "We're going to need all our energy today!"

I stopped halfway to the table and turned back around.

"What's that supposed to mean?"

"It's the day before Thanksgiving," she said. "You know what that means."

Of course. I'd forgotten because I try to block out this day from my memory every year.

"It's cleaning day!" she exclaimed. I couldn't tell if she was actually excited to clean or if she was just faking it.

I sighed. I should have known the bacon was a trick. Every year my mom forces the entire family to clean the house from top to bottom before our extended family shows up for Thanksgiving. Except that, really, it winds up being me and my dad who do all the work since Mom is usually busy prepping the food for the next day, and Jack and Ella aren't exactly the best cleaners.

My dad stalked into the kitchen and we looked at each other like soldiers entering a battlefield. We were resigned to our fate.

After breakfast, armed with Mom's *very* detailed instructions, we set out cleaning all sorts of places we usually never think about—beneath the fridge, along the baseboards, on top of doorframes, and even behind the toilets. Honestly, who on earth looks *there* for anything? Everyone knows that if something falls behind a toilet, whether it's a piece of toilet paper or a retainer, it's best left forgotten about for all of eternity.

Hours later, our elbows and backs screaming in agony, we passed out on the couch, completely exhausted. Before I knew it I'd drifted off to sleep again and found myself back on Loved Ones' Lane. Oddly, it wasn't as dark as usual. In fact, it was more of a peaceful sky blue, and it looked like only a sporadic few of the shooting stars were lit up. That made enough sense; just about everyone I knew would be awake this time of day.

I walked to the end of the lane to see if the ocean was there, and to my shock, the sun was out, and the water stretched as far as I could see.

Just there in the distance I could see the white capsized boat clearly, the two dark figures on top.

It was there again? Who kept having this bizarre dream? And why could I access it this way?

I dove in and swam through the water, which glittered so beautifully in the afternoon sun, like diamonds were encrusted in the waves.

Before I reached the boat, I heard singing. It was the guy, his voice smooth and velvety as he belted out "Amazing Grace." He clearly had a lot of practice.

> *I once was lost,*
> *but now I'm found*
> *'Twas blind,*
> *but now I see . . .*

"Hello?"

The singing immediately stopped.

"Who's there?" he said, his voice devastatingly hopeful.

"It's me, Baylor," I said, climbing to the top of the boat. "We just met the other day."

"Oh," he said, disappointed. Blisters covered his lips, all sore and bloody, and I found it amazing he could sing through that pain. "I thought I dreamed that."

"Well, you did," I said. "And I'd guess you're dreaming this now, too."

"Seems more like a nightmare."

"Your singing was great," I said. "Nothing nightmarish about that."

"I dreamed I was singing to my baby sister," he said. "She loves when I sing that. She plays peekaboo whenever I sing 'but now I see.'" He paused, and when he spoke next, his voice was heavy and cracking. "And now I don't know if I'll ever see her again."

"Why?" I asked.

"Because I'm stuck on this boat," he shouted, "in the middle of God knows where."

"But it's just a dream."

"It's not," he said, tears rolling down his dry, cracked skin. "It's not a dream. It's real."

And he must have woken up, because I suddenly popped back to the edge of the lane, the ocean scene gone once again.

When I woke up from my nap, I ran up to my room so I could tell Kristina everything.

"It doesn't make sense, though," she said. "Even if he was dreaming, you don't know this person. You shouldn't be able to visit his dreams."

"But I'm not really visiting them, not the way I do with everyone else. He comes to me."

"Even weirder, though. You can only channel spirits whose loved ones are nearby. We're not exactly close to the ocean."

"Right. I can only channel *spirits* whose loved ones are nearby. Maybe it's different with living people, though!"

She stared hard at the wall. "Right," she said. "Living people . . ."

"What is it?" I asked.

"I just think I need to chat with Fleetwood and some of the others about this," she said. "You're not really supposed to be channeling living people, just as a gentle reminder. It's not like anything I've heard of before." She eyed my shirt. "Make sure you keep wearing your amulet."

"Don't you think the amulet is what's causing this to happen, though?"

"Regardless, you're better off wearing it. Who knows what might happen if you wander off into this ocean without it?"

I turned the amulet over in my fingers. I was going to keep wearing it, but I couldn't help but feel concerned that a little stone was the one thing to keep me safe from any lurking dangers.

"All right," my mom said after walking through the house and running her finger along random surfaces to check for dust, "it's looking good, guys. Nice work."

My dad and I were sitting at the kitchen table, waiting for her seal of approval. We looked at each other and shook our heads.

"Every year," he mumbled.

"I'm actually impressed too," Kristina said, walking nearly lockstep with Mom. "There's a real shine to the place."

"Kristina also thinks we did a good job," I said.

Dad widened his eyes for a panicked split second before he composed himself. "Well, thank you, Kristina."

"No question where Jack gets his bravery from,"

she said sarcastically, sweeping past him and giving him a ghostly pat on the back, causing him to shiver.

Mom's phone beeped. "Oh, it's Glenn! Hello?"

Uncle Glenn is my mom's brother. We spend every Thanksgiving with him, his wife (my aunt Cathy), and their kids, Gillie and Oli. Gillie was a year older than me and had just started high school, and Oli was ten.

"Oh, he is? Oh . . . did he really? No, no, th-that's fine . . . Okay, we'll make up a bed for him then . . . See you tomorrow."

She hung up the phone and waited a moment before she said anything, like she was trying to figure out how to break terrible news.

"What'd he say, Connie?" Dad asked.

"Well," she said. "Cathy's dad missed his flight and now he doesn't feel like dealing with the airlines, so . . . so he's coming to dinner tomorrow."

A chill swept through the room.

"Horty is coming to Thanksgiving?" my dad said slowly.

"I'm sorry, honey," she said, "I know. What could I say?"

"How about, oh, I don't know . . . *hell no, Glenn, keep that monster out of my house!* And that's just off the top of my head, dear. Give me five more minutes and I'm sure I could get a lot more creative."

"It's Thanksgiving, Doug. I couldn't say no. Why not keep an open mind this year?"

"What am I missing?" I said, not sure I'd ever been more interested in anything in my entire life. "Why don't you like Horty?"

"That's family business, Baylor Douglas Bosco," my mom said sharply, "so don't you dare bring this up to your cousins, uncle, or, God forbid, your aunt."

I turned to Kristina and arched an eyebrow. She shook her head in equal confusion.

"Oh, no you don't," she said, flailing her arms around, as though she were swatting Kristina into pieces. "Don't you look at Kristina. And Kristina, if you know, don't you dare say a word, or so help me, I will remember this moment for my entire life, and when I finally meet you, first I'm going to hug you, but the second thing I'm going to do is ground you for the next eternity."

I looked from a very confused Kristina to a very frustrated Mom, then to a very annoyed Dad, and threw my hands up. "Now you have to tell me," I said. "What did he do?"

"We are going to have a *nice* day tomorrow," my mom said, as much to herself as to the rest of us, "and we are going to enjoy ourselves, and the food, and the company, and we're going to remember everything we have to be grateful for, even if it doesn't seem like there's a lot at the moment, and we're going to have a very . . . nice . . . time."

She stomped away, leaving Dad to fend off my questions. He was even more tight-lipped, though.

"Don't," he said, before I had the chance to say anything. "Just don't. Let it go."

Let it go? Did they not know me at all? I was going to find out what Horty did sooner or later, whether they liked it or not.

Kristina and I headed to the family room; I plopped on the couch, turned the TV on, and started rambling incessantly.

"How could we not know there was this weird dislike in the family. Horty? Don't I call him Uncle Horty? I think I've only met him a couple times before. What could he have possibly done to Dad?"

"He's not truly 'in the family,' though, is he? He's Mom's brother's wife's father. He's not blood, and there's no reason for you to ever see each other, really."

"Do you think he's got a door on Loved Ones' Lane?

She considered it for a moment. "If you can't think of any happy memories or significant moments with him, then I doubt it."

"Rats," I said. "I can't even do some reconnaissance work ahead of time."

"Well," she said, "not that I support your continued dreamwalking, but if you're going to do it anyway, tonight would be a good time to drop in on Mom and Dad. Maybe you'll see something there?"

I smiled. "Nice one. Maybe you should join me tonight."

She shook her head. "If they saw the two of us together, they would for sure know it was me, and not just some weird futuristic Ella."

I shrugged. "They don't know I can dreamwalk, though. They'll just think it's some weird dream if they spot us." I looked at the portrait of Kristina hanging on the wall above the TV, next to the school pictures featuring me, Jack, and Ella. "And now that they have the picture of you, it'd make sense if they started incorporating the two of us together in their dreams."

I'd made some friends at the police station after the whole Rosalie/Sheet Man debacle, and they'd hooked me up with a sketch artist who helped put together a solid composite of Kristina. It was only fair for Mom and Dad to have a reference point of what their long-lost daughter looked like.

"That's not the dumbest thing you've ever said, Baylor," she said. "I'll think about it."

Kristina was the kind of person—well, ghost—who

complimented me via positive negatives, so I took her words as the highest form of praise.

I was feeling pretty good about myself and grabbed the remote to put on something funny, but when I looked at the screen, my heart nearly rocketed up my esophagus and out my mouth.

"*The search-and-rescue mission for Helena Papadopoulos and Archie Perceval stretches into day five as the coast guard expands its search after weather experts say the volatile storm cells off the eastern seaboard may have carried any boat wreckage south. . . .*"

The image on the screen flashed from the stormy waters off the coast of Florida to school pictures of Helena and Archie. Chills washed over my body.

"Kristina," I said, my voice suddenly hoarse, "that's them. That's who I saw in my dream on the ocean."

There's *definitely* such a thing as bad publicity.

SHE LOOKED AT THE TV AND LISTENED TO the rest of the report. They lived on the east coast of Florida. They'd been missing since Friday afternoon. They'd taken Archie's dad's boat without permission. Not a single person had seen them since. The parents were asking for anyone with a plane or a boat to volunteer their time to look for their kids.

"That's who you saw in your dreams?" she asked. Her voice was sharp and steely.

I nodded. "Archie. I talked to him. He seemed delirious."

"I need to go." She disappeared in a flash of blue light, leaving me alone in the family room as Archie and Helena smiled at me from the TV.

The screen switched to footage of two sobbing women, one of whom was holding a little girl a year or two older than Ella.

"Please . . . please . . . if anyone knows anything, call the hotline," the one with the daughter said, her voice tinged with a Haitian accent. "We're desperate. We miss our babies." She broke into more heaving sobs as her daughter stared at her in confusion. I couldn't believe they were using this footage on TV.

The other woman was too distraught to say anything, and a big burly hand, its owner off-screen, was massaging one of her shoulders.

"How is this happening?" the first woman continued. "I never thought anything like this would happen to me."

"Baylor, what is that?" my mom asked, suddenly appearing in the family room. "Oh, turn that off! It's devastating." I flipped the TV off, trying to process what I was feeling. It was pure shock.

"That poor woman," my mom continued, sitting down next to me on the couch, gazing at me with wide eyes. "I can't imagine what she must be going through. She must feel like her soul's been torn into pieces." She shook her head. "Just horrible."

The words from the mother's interview's repeated themselves over and over in my head.

If anyone knows anything, call the hotline. We're desperate. We miss our babies.

I swallowed down vomit. I had to call that number immediately. Really, I had to head straight to Florida so I could help the parents figure out whether their kids were still alive or not. I needed to be in their proximity so the kids' ghosts could appear; that'd at least give them some kind of closure. But it was the day before Thanksgiving. What could I really do?

And . . . weren't they alive? Hadn't I seen them? Could what I'd experienced really have been a dream? It didn't make sense, though. If they were alive, then Kristina was right—I shouldn't have been able to access living people's dreams. What was the logic there? And if they were dead, I was too far from any of their loved ones for me to channel them.

They couldn't just show up whenever they pleased. That was one of the main rules Kristina had established with the other side. Otherwise billions upon billions of ghosts would try to access me all the time, trying to get me to deliver messages to the seven billion people scattered around the planet.

But the fact remained: I'd seen them somehow. And

for all I knew, they were still alive. If they were dead, they wouldn't have been lying on the boat so help-lessly. Unless Kristina was right about the oceans—what if they were worried about getting sucked away into the vastness of the sea, and they clung to the boat because it was the last vestiges of humanity they had left?

My head was throbbing. My heart was pounding. Why did Kristina have to leave so suddenly? I needed her help.

"Baylor?" my mom said cautiously. "Are you okay? You don't look so good."

"I . . . I, uh, I think I needed to lie down," I stammered.

"Oh no," she said. "Are you feeling sick?"

"No. I mean, yes, sort of, but don't worry, I'll be fine tomorrow," I managed to blurt.

"Baylor," she said, the caution in her voice replaced by suspicion, "is this a ghost thing?"

I nodded slowly.

"Got it," she said. She reached for the double-wick candle on the table and lit it up. "Do you need me to say anything or can you handle it?"

"I've got it," I said, and I imagined the light surrounding my body. It wasn't a necessary protection at the moment, but I was impressed my mom was trying to help in the first place, so I decided to go along with it.

"Let's get you upstairs," she said, putting my arm around her shoulders and grabbing me by the waist. "There we go. One step at a time."

We managed to get upstairs, and after I crawled into bed, she lit candles and placed them around the perimeter of my room.

"Thanks, Mom," I said as she tiptoed out.

"You're welcome, sweetie. Get some rest."

But I couldn't rest just yet. I needed to call the hotline. I found the number online and it went straight to a voice mail instructing me to leave a detailed message with my name and phone number.

"Uh, hi. My name is Baylor Bosco, and I can communicate with people who have crossed over. Except, sorry, no, I shouldn't have said that because I don't think your kids have crossed over. I guess I found another way to communicate with them, and I just wanted to tell you that they're both still alive and definitely lost at sea. They're lying on part of a shiny white boat. You need to find them soon, though, so please keep looking. Don't give up. Sorry. I wish I could be of more help." I left my phone number in case they wanted to call back, and I hung up.

I sighed with relief. I did my best to help, and now I could rest easy.

UPDATE: BAYLOR BOSCO'S DEVILISH DEEDS

It seems like a week can't go by without Keene's resident nuisance, Baylor Bosco, meddling in the lives of innocent people. After my special report from last week, I'm saddened to bring more news of Bosco's devilish exploits.

I'm told that Bosco attacked a group of second-graders shortly after purposely disrupting Keene's Thanksgiving Day Parade on Saturday morning.

"It seemed like an accident," said Mr. Gilbert, the band instructor at Keene Middle School. "I doubt he did it on purpose." Gilbert's judgment can understandably be called into question, however, thanks in large part to his hairstyle: a greasy mane of curly red hair.

After ruining his band's performance, Bosco then proceeded to attack a group of second-graders, with isolated reports stating he went so far as to set a demon after the kids.

"Who knows what that guy is capable of," reports my source, who wished to remain anonymous due to fear of any repercussions. "All I know is he scared my little brother to death."

Perhaps most shocking, though, is Bosco's most recent grab for attention. Sources tell me Bosco called the hotline for missing Floridian children Helena Papadopoulos and Archie Perceval, first saying the children had crossed over, and then retracting his claim, stating that the kids are still alive and he had somehow managed to communicate with them.

Needless to say, the parents of the missing children are not amused with Bosco's tricks—especially today, of all days, when our country is celebrating Thanksgiving. For someone whose job is to pass on healing messages, Bosco sure seems bent on causing as much pain as he possibly can.

—Carla Clunders, editor-at-large,

NewEnglandRealNews.net

"Stop it, Connie," Dad said calmly as he tried to grab my mom's phone out of her hands. "We don't have time for this. And it's Thanksgiving. We'll take care of it tomorrow. Just try to relax."

"Let go, Doug," she growled. "I need to track her down and kick her a—"

"Connie," he said through gritted teeth, "your younger son is now up and watching you behave this way."

She froze, turning her head to see Jack staring at her from the hallway leading into the kitchen.

"Happy Thanksgiving, honey," she sang, her voice unnaturally high.

"What's wrong?" Jack asked.

"Nothing, nothing," she said, letting Dad take the phone. She rushed over to Jack and guided him to join me at the table. "Cereal? Toast? What do you want to eat?"

"Toast, I guess."

"Coming right up!" she said frantically.

I could tell she was about to lose it. She'd been up since six, chopping and mixing and baking, and when I showed her Carla's new article, she went absolutely ballistic. I'd been obsessively checking that website twice a day and was horrified to a find an update this morning.

"That woman . . ." Mom muttered under her breath as she jammed two pieces of bread into the toaster so forcefully you'd have thought she had a personal vendetta against gluten. "Thinks she can write whatever she wants." She scoffed. "And on *Thanksgiving*? What monster raised her?"

Jack looked at me in confusion, and I just shook my head, feeling guilty. "Sorry, bro. Didn't mean to upset Mom on Thanksgiving. I keep messing things up for you."

She buttered the toast and threw it in front of Jack, who took small, tepid bites.

"Is the turkey ready to go in?" she asked Dad. "If it doesn't go in soon, we're going to be off schedule."

"Right," he said. "We have a schedule to stick to. Okay, just another minute. I need to finish stuffing it." He stared at her cell phone, and for a moment, I thought he was going to jam it into the turkey so my mom wouldn't be able to look at the article again or attempt to contact Carla Clunders. But he set it aside and reached for the bread and lemon peels.

"Everyone's arriving around one," Mom said. "Jack, you need to strip your bed and put on new sheets for Uncle Horty. He's sleeping in your room, and you'll have to sleep in Baylor's room."

"Oh, man," he said. "Why can't Baylor sleep in my room?"

"Because his room is bigger and your cousins need to fit in there too."

"Slumber party?" Jack said, his face lighting up.

Mom smiled. "Sure," she said. "Slumber party. Finish your toast and go fix up your room."

Jack wolfed down his toast and ran upstairs, leaving me alone at the table.

Mom was shaking her head at me. "That woman, Baylor. *Tomorrow*. Tomorrow I am going to track her down and tell her exactly what I think of her, and her journalistic integrity, and her . . . her . . . *stupid* website."

"Connie," my dad said quietly, a hint of warning in his voice.

She looked at him out of the corners of her eyes, and then glanced back at me.

Tomorrow, she mouthed, her eyes wide.

I nodded, giving her a thumbs-up.

"I'm going to shower," I said, heading upstairs. Really, I planned on reading the article ten more times. When I pulled up the website again, I was pleased to find a bunch of comments defending me.

Baylor4ever, 9:21 a.m.: Carla Clunders, you are a hack.

Writing inflammatory gossip articles about a 13yo boy? SAD.

BigBayliever11, 9:45 a.m.: Can you say "AGENDA"????? Clearly biased article. Amazing that Baylor was able to make contact with the missing kids. He is so blessed!!! Hope I can meet him soon, I miss my momma so much.

CamTheMan, 10:01 a.m.: the part with the anonymous source seemed really legit, Baylor scares kids for no reason, what a weirdo.

I rolled my eyes. The last commenter was clearly Cam Nguyen. How on earth had she tracked him down for this nonsensical article? No, seriously, could this even be called an article? It sounded like a flame piece written by one of my classmates trying really hard to seem like a grown-up.

I read over a few more comments, embarrassed by the different usernames that incorporated part of my name. I knew there were people who called themselves Baylievers, but I didn't think they were rabid enough to be defending me on random news articles.

I searched for "Baylor Bosco Bayliever" and was shocked to discover the first result was for a website called BaylieversUnited.com. I clicked on it, and my cheeks burned. An image of me popped up. It looked like a screenshot from one of the news segments that'd aired shortly after the Sheet Man incident. I was looking off into the distance, focusing hard on something, and my arm was raised, with my hand turned up slightly, fingers spread evenly apart. It looked like I was performing a magic spell.

The home page looked like some sort of message board, with several different threads.

RECENT NEWS

SHARE YOUR EXPERIENCE

PRESS

PHOTOS/VIDEOS

I clicked on RECENT NEWS, and the Carla Clunders update was the first one listed. I glanced down and saw there'd been a crazy hubbub of activity the last few weeks, with all sort of different articles posted about Rosalie and Alfred.

I clicked on the post about this morning's article. There were already seventeen comments on it.

OhioMom1212: Baylor is THIRTEEN and so gifted. It must be such a burden for him sometimes to have so much power. I can't imagine.

TranscendentXX: She seems like a pleasant woman . . . NOT!

GhostBoy11: sounds like a mean jerk to me, he should

just mind his own business

BondedByond1980: Wonder if he delivered a message

she didn't like and now she's out to get him. Poor

kid. He helps so many people, doesn't deserve this

treatment.

I was happy to see the vast majority of comments were in my defense. I guess it wouldn't make sense for a lot of people to hang out on a website called BaylieversUnited.com if they weren't actually united. Well, unless they were united in their dislike of me.

Part of me wondered if there was an opposite forum somewhere on the web—some sort of hate site, like BaylorsABrat.com, and it would just be a bunch of people talking about how they thought I was a fraud and hoodwinking people left and right. I didn't bother to check, though. That kind of negative energy was the last thing I needed.

I'd nearly forgotten I had to shower and clean my room, so I jumped into high gear and did everything I needed to do in less than twenty minutes. Jack slinked into my room and rolled out his sleeping bag on the opposite side of the room from my bed.

"Oli and Gillie can have the middle," he said, smoothing out the top part.

Kristina and Colonel Fleetwood materialized out of nowhere, and I jumped back, not expecting them to pop up so suddenly. Jack looked up and frowned.

"What is it?" he asked.

"Nothing," I said, catching my breath. "Kristina just surprised me."

Jack's face fell a little more. "Oh," he said. "I forgot my pillow." He slinked out of the room.

"What's his problem?" Kristina asked.

"Everyone's a little on edge today," I said. "Carla posted another article, and Mom's not happy. And when Mom's not happy, no one's happy."

"She's the best," Kristina said with an adoring sigh.

"She really is a delightful woman," the colonel said.

But I didn't know what to say, because my attention was squarely focused on the uninvited ghost standing behind them, hunched over and staring back at me with shadowy eyes.

12

Do NOT let old people sit on your hand.

"KRISTINA," I WHISPERED, MY VOICE HOARSE. I reached slowly and steadily for the candle and lighter on my desk. "Colonel. Don't panic."

The colonel cocked his head to the side, curious, and followed my gaze past his shoulders.

"Oh, apologies, Baylor," he said with a hearty laugh. He had bright brown eyes that somehow seemed to shimmer vibrantly when he laughed, and Kristina always stared and smiled at him like she couldn't get enough of looking at them. It was really annoying. "We should have mentioned this first thing. You have a visitor!"

He took a step to the side to reveal a short man with matted gray hair and the complexion of a wild mushroom that desperately needed to be cleaned. His stance was a bit lopsided and gave the impression he was in danger of falling over, as though his left leg was four inches too short. He was attempting a grin, but it looked more like he had some gas-related discomfort.

"Uhh," I mumbled. "Hello?"

"Baylor Bosco," he said, his voice at once smooth and raspy, like an old-fashioned jazz singer's. "A pleasure to see ya."

"I'm sure I'd like to say the same," I said.

"Baylor," Kristina said sharply. "This is your great-great-great-grandpa Charlie."

"A bit long, that name, innit?" he said. A light accent that I couldn't place lingered at the end of his words. "My friends—back when I was still walking around on your side, I mean—they always called me Ten-Buck Chuck." He smiled proudly. "Always up for a ten-dollar bet. Wha's ten bucks at the end of the day, really? Was a good way to pass the time on the docks, if anything."

"I'd imagine it was a lot of money back when you were alive," I said, shrugging. "Probably could have paid half your rent or something with it."

"Nah, don' be silly, Baylor," he said, stepping past Kristina and the colonel. "Let me get a good look at ya in the light."

"Okay?" I said, suddenly wondering what to do with my hands as he looked me up and down. "What are you doing here, uh, Ten-Buck Chuck?"

He chuckled. "Jus' Charlie works fine too." He seemed fixated on my legs. "We've gotten taller through the years, we O'Briens, haven' we?" He nodded with approval. "Probably needed to jus' survive in these big new cities. That Darwin knew what he was talking about. Won' shut up about it these days, mind ya, and sometimes to rile him up, I'll say, 'Hey, Charles'—see, he's a bit of a snot, goes by *Charles* and all—so I'll say, 'Hey *Charles*, isn' it just a *theory*, though? Nothing actually proven, right?'" His eyes lit up and he slapped his hands together. "Ya should see his reaction! Blabbers on and on and on, as if any of us really care."

I gawked at him, entirely speechless.

"Charlie decided to join us for Thanksgiving this year," Kristina said through gritted teeth. "He is family, after all."

He motioned as if he were tipping down the brim of a hat. "Might get some of the other family members to show up, too, but you never know on Thanksgiving. Busy travel day and all, things get crowded."

"Crowded?" I scoffed. "You're ghosts! What does that matter?"

"It doesn't matter," Kristina said, glaring at Charlie, who smiled back at her in confusion.

"Wait, do you——?" I began, but Kristina cut me off.

"We have other things to discuss, Baylor," she said quickly. "Namely the fact that you're seeing the dreams of a couple random kids who are drifting somewhere thousands of miles away."

I immediately thought of the grim scene with Helena and Archie, their weak, thin bodies battered by the sun and the waves.

"What'd you find out?"

"Well, it's not particularly good since——"

"Baylor!" my mom shouted from downstairs. "Your uncle just called. They're getting here early. Come down and help me set up the kitchen!"

"One second!" I shouted back. "Okay, go ahead, Kristina."

"So they're——"

"We do not have *one second*, Baylor Douglas Bosco!" she screamed up again. "Get your butt down here right now before I come up there and drag you to this kitchen by your ears."

"Oh, I like her," Charlie said. "Is she an O'Brien? She sounds like one."

Kristina nodded.

"This is going to be a fun evening," Charlie said.

I sighed. "Coming!"

I marched downstairs and found my mom whirling in the kitchen, my dad attempting to set up the long table, and my brother, who never returned to my room with a pillow, keeping Ella busy in the family room.

"Help your father," she said, her face covered in a bit of flour and some type of yellowish mashed vegetable. "He needs it."

"I don't *need* it," he said through gritted teeth, "but I can't get this thing to snap!" He was banging on one of the metal legs, trying to get a clasp to click into place.

"Let Baylor try," she said.

I walked over and shook the table a little while the trio of ghosts lingered around us and looked over our shoulders.

"See?" Dad said triumphantly. "It's stuck."

"It looks like the left side is a bit dented, Baylor," the colonel said, peering over the table, his body bent at the most awkward angle I'd ever seen any ghost attempt. Certainly no human could ever mimic it, at least not without sustaining serious injury; he was nearly at a perfect right angle, bending from the middle of his thighs as though they contained hinges. "Try pressing hard on that side while you pull it down."

I followed his advice and the clasp snapped into place.

"It worked!" I yelped, and I smiled at the colonel, who was nodding his approval, before I coughed and looked away.

"Yeah, well, that's because I sat here loosening it for ten minutes," Dad grumbled, more to the clasp than to me.

"You tried, Doug," Mom said. "Now put the table-cloths on, line up the runner down the middle—make sure it's not crooked!—set the table, put out the flowers and candles, and then help me wipe down the counters."

Dad and I looked at each other and sighed. "I wonder if we can escape unnoticed to the Kirkwoods for pizza?" I said quietly.

"Son," he said just as quietly, "neither one of us is talented enough to pull one over on your mother."

After a frantic hour of setting up and last-minute cleaning ("You checked behind the toilets, right,

Baylor?" my mom had shrieked at one point), we heard Jack announce that Uncle Glenn's car had pulled into the driveway.

"They're here!" Mom yelled from the kitchen.

"Yeah, we know, Jack just said so," I said, confused.

She turned my way, her face freshly cleaned of random kitchen residue, arched an eyebrow, and wordlessly assessed me, her eyes wide and threatening. I gulped, and she continued to stare for a few more seconds.

"Mom?" I said, wondering if I was about to get grounded for some unknown reason.

The sound of a knock pierced the air, and she suddenly smiled, the dark look disappearing from her face and the chaos and stress of the morning dissolving from her mind. "It's Thanksgiving time!" she sang, her voice the cheeriest it had been all day. She rushed to the front door and opened it to find Uncle Glenn holding three large casserole dishes and a huge bag slung around his back. Next to him, my cousin Gillie smiled in a forced way, like someone had placed hooks in the corners of her mouth and pulled hard. Behind them, Aunt Cathy and my other cousin, Oli, were futzing with something in the backseat.

"Glenny!" Mom said, going in for a hug but realizing a second too late it was an impossible task with everything he was holding. She wound up tenderly caressing the aluminum foil of the casserole dishes before she stepped back and said, "Come in, come in!"

"Thanks, baby sis," he said, crossing the threshold and disappearing into the kitchen. Gillie followed him, but Mom pulled her in for a hug, much to the dismay of Gillie, who stood motionless as my mom tightly squeezed her arms around her. For the second time in less than ten seconds, Mom appeared to be hugging an inanimate object, and she was fully aware of it.

She released Gillie after an awkward few seconds, clapped her hands together, and said, "How are you, my beautiful niece? Are you liking high school? Made lots of new friends?"

Gillie stared back at her, tugging at her straight, shiny brunette hair, but looking like she wanted to wrap it around her neck and pull until she didn't have to talk anymore.

"It's fine," she said, her voice different than I remembered it, now a bit slower and higher. "You know. It's . . . good."

Mom nodded. "Great!" she said. "I can't wait to hear all about it." She looked at me and said, "Say hello to your cousin, Baylor!"

I looked from Mom to Gillie and was unsure of what to do. It seemed like a better idea to shake her hand or give her a casual pat on the back, but I knew my mom wouldn't be happy with that, so I endured the same fate as my mom and found myself hugging what felt like a very thin, bony pole.

"Nice to see you, Gillie," I said, letting go, my cheek feeling sort of greasy from where it'd touched her face, like a whole bottle of lotion had exploded on her skin. "Ready for our slumber party?"

Uncle Glenn reappeared at the moment, free of dishes and bags, and Gillie looked at her dad, a flash of anger crossing her face.

"I thought you were joking about the sleeping bags," she said, annoyed.

"Why would I kid about the sleeping bags?" he asked.

"Are you kidding me?" Gillie asked, her voice rising. "A sleeping bag on Baylor's floor? That type of accommodation is not acceptable."

Uncle Glenn turned his head a bit and stared at her, his expression eerily similar to mom's from just moments ago. "You know what's not acceptable, Gillie?" he said. "That snotty tone of yours. Say one more word about it and I'll make sure you sleep on the kitchen floor with a dish towel for a pillow."

She glared at him. "That's child abuse."

He smiled. "That's parenting. Take your stuff up to Baylor's room. *Now.*"

She stomped upstairs and he turned back to my mom, who looked at him with a face of admiration. "Happy Thanksgiving," he said sarcastically, imitating Gillie's voice. "I'm sooo thankful for high school. It's, *like*, the best."

Mom laughed and finally gave him a proper hug. "Everyone goes through it," she said, her head on his shoulder. "I remember being a fourteen-year-old and feeling so insecure and trying to fit in. Girls are so mean, too." She let go of him, frowned, and shook her head. "Much meaner than boys. It's tough."

I got a cold feeling in the pit of my stomach. I started high school next year, and seeing Gillie act like that and hearing Mom talk about it made me nervous.

"Yeah, well, things are different these days," he said. "You didn't have cell phones or computers or *social media.*" He made a face like he'd taken cough syrup. "She's been in high school for less than three months and it's like an alien spaceship sucked her up, messed with her brain, and spit down this creature I don't recognize." Mom looked at me quickly, a note of panic crossing her face, before turning back to her brother. He didn't notice, though, because he'd turned to me. "Or, hey, maybe a demon's haunting her, Baylor. Any chance you can perform an exorcism this weekend?"

I attempted a meek laugh. "Probably not," I said. "I'll go help Gillie with her bag."

"Well, before you do that, would you mind helping your aunt with her stuff? Her father's a bit of, uh, a handful," he stammered, looking at my mom. "Sorry again about all that."

"It's fine," she said, her tone breezy. "Don't even think about it."

"Yeah, but I know Doug—"

"It's fine," she said sharply, and it was clear they wouldn't be discussing it again.

It took all the strength I had to shove the bubbling questions back down my throat. I looked at Kristina, who shrugged, just as stumped. Annoyed, I grabbed my jacket and headed out to the car.

Oli, a few years younger than me, was balancing a perilous stack of bags in his arms. "Hi, Baylor," he said, enthusiasm bursting out of his pores.

"The boy's aura is golden," the colonel exclaimed. "Wow!"

"He's obsessed with Baylor," Kristina said, "and he fights with Jack because he's so jealous Jack has an older brother." She looked at me sadly. "Though

it seems like Jack would be perfectly willing to trade places with Oli."

"We're going to fix that," I whispered from the corner of my mouth before turning back to Oli. "Hey, Oli. Hey, Aunt Cathy," I said.

Aunt Cathy didn't respond because she was half inside the backseat of the car, fumbling around with something.

"What's she doing?" I asked Oli.

"Grandpa's fussing over his seat belt. Keeps saying it's stuck."

"Do they need help?"

"No," he said, rolling his eyes. "He's just sitting on it and won't move over to unbuckle it."

"What's his name again? Horty?"

"Yeah, lots of people call him Uncle Horty," he said.

"Got it," I said, eyeing his bags, which seemed to teeter left and right more and more with each passing second. "Those look heavy. Go inside; I'll help your mom."

Oli walked toward the house, and I went to the other side of the car, opened the door, and stuck my head in. Immediately an unwelcome cloud of pungent, spicy cologne invaded my nose. I covered my nose and mouth, hoping to filter the foul scent. Uncle Horty sat in the middle seat, his arms dangling helplessly as his daughter had her hands buried beneath his body.

"Aunt Cathy?" I said.

"Oh, hi, Baylor," she said, looking up. "Sorry, just trying to help my dad with his seat belt. Dad, you remember Baylor, of course." She forced an odd laugh. "And Baylor, feel free to call him Uncle Horty."

Uncle Horty's body looked like a collection of rectangles and squares. He had broad, sharp shoulders that blended seamlessly with his wide torso, and his legs stuck out on both sides of the middle console at a perfect perpendicular angle. His head was oddly small compared to the rest of his body, but it was just as sharp and angular, like it had been sculpted using a shoe box as a guide.

"Hello, Baylor," he said, his voice higher than I thought it was going to be. "I'd shake your hand, but we're a little preoccupied at the moment."

"Dad, all you have to do is scoot forward a little and I can unbuckle it," Aunt Cathy said, her exasperation more than evident. It sounded like that was the twentieth time she'd repeated the same sentence.

"Cathy, dear, it's *stuck*," he said, enunciating the last word slowly and condescendingly.

"Oh, this is just pathetic," Kristina said, watching

from the passenger seat as Charlie and the colonel stood nearby.

"It's not stuck," Aunt Cathy said. "You're just not used to these new cars with small middle seats. If you'd just sat in the front like I'd asked you to, this wouldn't have been a problem."

"I like the backseat," he said simply. "I get a good view of the road and can help the driver out."

"Yes, and while Glenn thoroughly appreciated your desire to help, it's probably best to just let the driver drive next time."

"Oh no, you can never be too careful, Cathy, not these days," he said with all the concern of a doctor explaining that the bubonic plague had returned and we were all doomed. "You never know what pyschos are out on the roads anymore, swerving left and right, drunk at ten in the morning, wreaking havoc on the innocents of the world."

Cathy sighed. "You're going to be stuck here all day if you don't sit up," she said. "We're not going to cut this seat belt just because you don't understand how it works."

"Maybe we should call a mechanic," he suggested.

"Baylor," she said suddenly, jerking her head in my direction, her short hair flying waywardly around her head, "give me your belt."

"What?"

"Your belt," she said. "Take it off and give it to me."

Uncle Horty and I looked at each other in confusion as I took off the belt. Was she about to choke him to death? If that were the case, I wouldn't let her go through with it, of course, but I was semicurious to see her make the attempt.

"Bet she chokes him," Charlie said with delight. "Any takers?"

She grabbed my belt, fastened it around her dad's legs, and told me to come to her side. She grabbed my shoulders and leaned forward as her dad hummed helplessly from the inside the car.

"I'm going to hoist him up in a second, and you're going to dig in there, find the buckle, and *click it*," she said in a way that suggested she might morph into a snake and swallow me whole if I didn't succeed the first time.

"Got it," I said. We turned to the car, squeezed in, and got into position, my body angled awkwardly under hers. She pulled up on the belt, shifting her father up and away from the seat. I shoved my hands under his legs, searching for the buckle, hoping beyond hope he hadn't had an accident or something during the car ride. My right hand found the end of the belt, and I yelped with excitement as I plunged my finger into the red button and the belt suddenly loosened and zoomed against the seat.

Aunt Cathy let go of the belt and Uncle Horty landed hard on the seat, as did my hands, which were unfortunately still on the buckle. We both screamed at the same time—he in pain, and me because my hands were touching an old man's butt. I yanked my hands away, forgetting Aunt Cathy was positioned awkwardly over me, and I accidentally elbowed her in the face.

She screamed as well, and we both fell backward out of the car and onto the pavement in a heap.

"Are you okay?" I asked, lifting myself off her.

"I think so," she said, clutching her eyebrow as my mom, dad, and uncle ran out of the house to see what was going on after hearing three separate screams. "Just missed my eye, thankfully."

"What happened?" my dad asked, the first to arrive, surveying the scene.

"These modern cars," Uncle Horty said, sliding gracefully out of the car and stepping over Aunt Cathy and me. "Only a fool would believe they're safer than ever. Clearly not." He pointed to us on the ground as if to prove his point.

My dad bent down to help us get on our feet.

"Oh, Cathy, you're bleeding," he groaned. His

hands awkwardly hovered over a cut just above her eyebrow, unsure of what to do.

"See?" Uncle Horty said. "This never would have happened in the seventies."

"Oh, really, Horty?" Dad spit, glowering at the old man. "Yeah, those cars were *so* much safer, you know, without all the air bags and seat belts and pumping breaks and alarm systems."

As my dad finished his little speech, Uncle Horty smirked. "Happy Thanksgiving, Douglas. It's good to see you again."

My dad opened his mouth to say something, but my mom touched his shoulder and walked forward to embrace the old man in a hug.

"Great to see you, Horty. Now let's get your daughter inside before that cut gets infected."

She grabbed Aunt Cathy around the shoulder and led her inside the house, leaving me, my dad, Uncle Glenn, Uncle Horty, and a trio of ghosts to awkwardly stare at one another in the driveway.

"Well," Charlie piped up, his voice eager and excited, "looks like we're goin' to be in for a very interesting evening!"

13

Spelling matters.

BACK INSIDE THE HOUSE, THE KIDS WERE all settled in the family room as the adults putzed around in the kitchen.

"Mom and Dad will be here closer to dinner," Mom said to Uncle Glenn. "Aunt Hilda's taking her sweet time getting ready."

"Of course she is," chirped Uncle Horty from the table. I wondered if Aunt Hilda and Uncle Horty had ever spent a long time with each other. Surely their paths had crossed here and there at various family events, but it seemed like a disaster waiting to happen, like two storms set to converge into a hurricane of unpleasantness.

"Ella, Ellllla, *Ellllllllaaaa*," sang Oli, who was playing with Ella in front of the TV. She was chucking blocks at his head, and he was swatting them away.

"Oli, seriously?" Gillie said from the couch. "Could you be more annoying?"

"Oh, sorry I'm playing with our baby cousin, Gillie!" he said back. "Sorry I actually want to spend time with my family."

She rolled her eyes. "You can spend time with the family and not be such an annoying freak at the same time," she said.

"Do you think I'm an annoying freak, Ella? Do youuu, Ellaaaa?" he said.

"Oli!" Aunt Cathy snapped from the kitchen, a bright pink Band-Aid over her eyebrow. "Don't say that word in front of Ella!"

"What word?"

"'Freak!' We don't want her learning words like that."

"She's never going to remember that word," he said. "It's not even that bad of a word."

"Did I ask you for your parenting advice, Oli? No. I didn't. Have you raised two children and know what's best for them? No. You haven't. Don't say that word again."

I looked at Kristina and snickered. She and the colonel were leaning against the wall near the kitchen, so they could hear each conversation perfectly. Charlie was sitting at the kitchen table next to Uncle Horty, inches away from his face, studying his every wrinkle.

I motioned in their direction to Kristina. She glanced at them and grimaced.

"Charlie, what are you doing?" she asked.

"How is his skin so tight for such an old man?"

Kristina and I heard a commotion from the other side, and I made a face at her. I hadn't even realized I was tuned out. I didn't think much about it at home thanks to the various protections in place. I squeezed the amulet under my shirt, amazed at how quickly it had helped me.

"I think . . . I think that's Horty's sister," she said.

"It's his wife," the colonel corrected her.

"She's complaining at the moment. Delivering a message, ironically, from the other ghosts wanting to deliver a message. Saying you've been tuning them out too much recently. They haven't had a chance of getting through." Kristina smiled. "I think that means the amulet has really been helping you, though. But, oh wow, she's a talker. Going on about how it's your life's purpose to deliver healing messages to help people, not to spend all your time traipsing around other people's dreams like some kind of Peeping Tom." She rolled her eyes. "Listen, lady, Baylor can deliver any and all messages at his discretion."

I could hear the woman talking back in the same way you might hear a muffled conversation through the thin walls of a cheap hotel.

"Well, if you don't like it, you can take that up with the Higher Powers," Kristina growled back, her body highlighted in a faint blue glow, growing more intense as she said every furious word. "Quite frankly, your opinion has as much value as a pile of demon dung, and if you want to have even a glimmer of a chance of Baylor delivering your message to Horty, I suggest you silence yourself now."

By the time she finished, she was hovering several inches off the ground, illuminated in a swirling blue energy that eagerly lapped off her in flares and bursts, like she was commanding a small but vigorous ocean. The light slowly faded away, and she sank back to the earth, looking a bit embarrassed as she tucked a piece of hair behind her ear.

"Now *that's* an O'Brien woman!" Charlie hollered, standing up from the table and pointing at Kristina. "That's it, girl. You tell 'em!"

Kristina couldn't blush, but had she been alive, she would have been burning red from Charlie's compliments and the colonel's proud smile.

"Baylor, *what* are you doing?" Gillie said from behind her phone.

"Huh?"

"You're totally spazzing!" she said, sounding interested for the first time all day. She put down her phone and looked at me in amazement. "Was that . . . were you just . . . ?"

Now it was my turn to blush. "Oh, sorry," I said. "I'm so used to talking to ghosts at home. Sorry if I made you uncomfortable."

"Are you kidding?" she said. "Was . . . was that"— her voice dropped to a whisper—"was that Kristina?"

I looked at her overly made-up face, her cheeks shiny and pink, her eyes dark with ashy blue shadow, and I nodded. "Yeah."

She squealed. "Oh wow," she said. "That was so cool. My friends are going to *freak!*"

"Gillie!" Aunt Cathy barked. "What did I just say to your brother about that word?"

"Sorry," she said, looking at her mom and sounding zero percent sorry. "But Baylor was just channeling Kristina, and it was awesome." She turned back to me. "You have no idea, Baylor, but my friends think you're, like, the coolest person ever. When they found out I was your cousin, they nearly *died.*" She covered her mouth and giggled. "Oh, sorry. I didn't mean to say that. But you know what I mean. My friend Erin is, like, the biggest Bayliever around." My cheeks burned. "She checks this crazy website all the time, BaylieversUnited.com, have you heard of it?"

Somehow, my cheeks burned more, hot enough to make a pan sizzle.

"Um, yeah, I have," I said.

"Apparently some lady has been posting articles about you. Did you know that?" she said, her eyes wide and hopeful. "Have you read them?"

"Yeah," I said. "She's not a very good reporter, though."

"Oh, totally not," Gillie said. "But still, it's pretty cool having people write about you."

My mom must have noticed me nearly drowning in my own saliva because she chimed in to pivot the conversation in another direction.

"Have you guys seen Baylor's gifts for us?" she said happily, though I could tell from the shape of her eyes that she was slightly concerned for me. "I'll show you the one outside first! Follow me."

She led the way to the backyard through the door by the kitchen table. Uncle Horty stayed put, saying he was still feeling a bit too fragile to move, but everyone else went out to see the stone I had made to mark Kristina's presence in the world. It'd bothered me that she was such a big part of our lives but there was nothing to indicate as much. With the help of Madame Nadirah, I'd commissioned a memorial stone that read: *For Kristina, our beloved daughter and sister, whose love lives on in our hearts.*

"I hate to ask," Aunt Cathy said, "but how did . . . how did she get named?"

"I don't know, actually," I said. "It just kind of happened." I turned to Kristina. "I think you said Mom was going to name me Kristina if I'd been a girl, so the glove just sort of fit, I guess."

"That's true," Mom said, her voice high. "Yes. Of course, I wouldn't have spelled it that way, though. I would have spelled it *Christina*, with a *C*."

"Wait," I said. "What?"

"I have no idea where the *K* came from," Mom said, shrugging. "It kind of fits, though. It makes the name seem . . . oh, I don't know . . . mystical?"

"That's not what we were going for," I said, looking at Kristina in shock. She looked a bit dazed herself, actually. Charlie, standing behind her, had his fist over his mouth, stifling his laughter. "I think . . . it just made more sense with a *K* when I was younger!"

Charlie burst into laughter.

"The O'Briens aren't the smartest men around, I'll

give you that much," he said through his giggles, slapping his knee. "I'll give you that much."

"Shut up, Charlie!" I said, feeling horrible. "Sorry, Kristina. I had no idea."

Jack, who'd been standing next to me, suddenly lunged away, realizing ghosts were nearby.

She shrugged. "It really doesn't matter. I never write my name anyway."

"Who's Charlie?" Mom asked.

"Don't ask," I said, crossing my arms across my chest. "It's freezing. Let's go back inside."

Charlie, through his laughter, sputtered, "Y-you'd never know it was freezing, based on those—those burning cheeks of yours, kiddo!"

Once we'd resettled inside the house, we somehow still had another hour to kill before dinner was served at four. Gillie turned the TV on and started flipping through the channels while Jack and I lazily watched it. Oli and Ella had moved on to coloring, which really meant that Oli had to repeatedly pluck crayons out of her mouth as she tried to suck on each one. Meanwhile, the adults had opened the first bottle of red wine and were sitting around the table catching up.

It was pretty boring for a while until Gillie flipped to a random news channel, and Jack, Gillie, and I

gasped at the same time. A big photo of me was staring back at us from the screen.

"What is it?" Mom said, standing up and running
over to look at the TV, wineglass still in hand.

> ". . . the young man from Keene, New Hampshire,
> who claims to have the ability to talk to dead
> people. He's made headlines in recent weeks for
> his involvement in the disappearance of Rosalie
> Timmons, and he's making headlines again for
> his involvement in the missing persons case of
> Helena Papadopoulos and Archie Perceval, the
> teenagers from Florida who are believed to be
> missing at sea for several days now . . ."

"No!" Mom shrieked, spilling wine down her hand
and across the hardwood floor. "Off! Off! Off!"
Gillie fumbled with the remote, desperately trying
to find the power button after her aunt had yelled at
her for the first time ever. Meanwhile, I was sitting
in shock after seeing my face pop up on TV—on a
national news channel, no less.

Aunt Cathy rushed to the room with a roll of
paper towels. She wiped off Mom's hand first before

crouching to mop up the liquid on the floor. Mom was also in shock, trying to make sense of not only seeing her son on the national news (again), but also having a son who possessed a gift so beyond her ability to comprehend that she was paralyzed altogether.

I turned to Dad. "You should refill Mom's glass," I said, my voice colder than ice.

He seemed confused, not having seen or heard the news report, but he grasped my tone and quickly got up, wine bottle in hand, to replenish the glass and guide her back to the kitchen. Uncle Horty stared at me, his expression pleasant but curious, while Aunt Cathy and Uncle Glenn pretended nothing had happened at all.

Jack, his eyebrows nearly to his hairline, was staring at me like I was a ghost, while Gillie was smirking at me with a mix of admiration and jealousy. Oli had ignored the whole scene thanks to Ella's Crayola craving.

Thankfully, Grandma Renee and Grandpa By decided to show up with Aunt Hilda not a moment too late. The ring of the doorbell cut through the silence, and I hopped up.

"I'll get it," I yelped.

I ran to the door and threw it open to find the three of them staring at me happily.

"Happy Thanksgiving!" Grandma Renee said, holding a crumbly apple pie in her hands. "Are you ready to eat?"

I shook my head. "I think everyone's ready to throw up, actually."

Be thankful you're not in my family.

GRANDMA FROWNED AT ME. "WHAT'S WRONG?"

"It's kind of a long story, but some woman's been writing nasty articles about me, and then my face was *just* on the national news and Mom made a scene out of it, and Uncle Horty's a weirdo, and Gillie's being a jerk because she's in high school," I said in one breath.

Grandpa By surged past his wife and enveloped me in a gigantic bear hug.

"It's not an easy thing, being this talented, but the O'Briens have been talented for generations, Baylor. Generations! That's centuries and centuries of talent,

talent of all different shades and colors, and it's a burden to bear at times, yes, it's a burden." He nodded vigorously. "Believe me, *I* get it, but we persevere! We keep going, and we push past the problem, and we face it head on, because we are O'Briens and that is just what we do."

"Yes!" yelped Charlie, entering the foyer from the kitchen and clapping loudly. "Now *this* is a true O'Brien!" He reached up to his head and motioned, yet again, as though he were tipping a hat. "Byron O'Brien, my great-grandson. I'd recognize an aura like that anywhere."

"Grandpa," I said, as he let me go, "do you know who Charlie O'Brien is?"

Grandpa narrowed his eyes. "Charlie O'Brien? My great-great-grandpa? Of course I do. Never met him; he died before I was born, but I know he was a sailor and once remember hearing he was something of a keen crook. Pick-pocketing anyone he could get within a foot of. Apparently everyone called him One-Buck Chuck because he'd steal even one buck if he could get his grubby hands on it."

"Oy!" Charlie said. "First things first, tha's just a bit rude, innit? My hands aren't grubby."

I rolled my eyes.

"Secondly, tha's all a lie! Generations of reputation mismanagement! I told ya the truth before. They called me *Ten*-Buck Chuck, because I was daring enough to do anything for ten bucks."

"I thought you said it was because you were always up for a bet," Kristina said.

"Tomato, *tomahto!*" he said. "I'm not a crook. Look at me!"

He somehow seemed dirtier and more lopsided than before, and Kristina and I exchanged uncertain glances.

"Maybe it'd be best to keep your head down for a bit, Charlie," the colonel suggested.

Aunt Hilda looked me up and down as she hobbled through the doorway, shaking her head.

"It's that pesky ghost business, isn't it?" she said. "I had a dream about my friend Marge the other day"—she glanced at me pointedly—"I'm sure you remember her. We were playing bunco, and she mentioned you, funny enough. Told me to be nicer to you! As if I'm not nice to you already!" She laughed and started hacking into a handkerchief. "Anyway," she said after she stopped coughing, "it was nice to see her, even if it was only a dream."

Grandma Renee was staring at me funny as her sister was speaking. "I had a dream about you, too, Baylor," she said, shaking her head. "It was nothing. Just some dumb dream. But . . . it was just . . . so . . ." She extended her hand and touched my face. "So realistic."

As she studied my face, my mom came into the foyer, a very full wineglass in her hand, and said, "Mom! Dad! Auntie! Happy Thanksgiving!"

Grandpa By chuckled. "Happy Thanksgiving to you, too, my doll," he said. "Thank you for hosting us once again."

"Of course," she said, and when she spoke next, her voice was lowered slightly, her smile thin. "Uncle Horty has joined us this year."

Grandma Renee straightened her back. "Yes, Glenn let us know," she said icily. "I'm sure Doug was thrilled to find out."

"What did he do?" I asked quickly before I could stop myself.

The four of them stared at me, their eyebrows raised, their mouths slightly open, before glancing at one another.

"Never you mind, dear, it's ancient history," Grandma Renee said, wrapping her arm around my shoulder and guiding me forward. "Now where are my other grandchildren? We need to get a picture of the five of you together! Grandma needs a new profile picture!"

After everyone had greeted and hugged and kissed one another, it was time to set out the casseroles, carve the turkey, and shovel food into our mouths for dinner.

"Baylor," Mom said over the buzz of the electric knife as she separated a drumstick from the turkey, "want to get the candles?"

"I'm on it!" I said, grabbing the matches to light the candlesticks placed along the tables. Mom made sure to always have candles at every party she threw because they added both ambience and protections. No offense to potpourri or flowers or those weird tea doily things, but if you can't look nice *and* ward off evil spirits, then what's the point, really?

The adults popped a bottle of champagne while the kids, who had sparkling apple cider and grape juice to sip on, went first to get food.

"It's so good to see everyone," said Uncle Glenn, holding up his glass to toast with the others.

"It sure is," Aunt Hilda said, before turning directly to Horty. "Even you, Horty." She was seated directly across from him, on the side furthest from the kids' table that Dad and I had assembled earlier in the day. It jutted out as an extension of the main kitchen table, and the whole thing resembled something like a giant lollipop. She tilted her glass in his direction, and he raised an eyebrow, reaching across the table with his glass. *Clink.*

A brief, intense silence followed as Horty and Hilda stared at each other and sipped from their glasses.

"You youngsters!" Grandpa By said, trying to laugh it off.

"You might think me insane," whispered the colonel, "but I have a feeling they don't like each other." There wasn't enough room for the ghosts at the tables if they'd been human, but somehow they managed to squeeze in with plenty of room right at the gaps where the kids' table met the adults' table.

"The British guy's smart," Charlie said across from me, rolling his eyes. "He must have talked to, what, more than four people in his lifetime to have the people skills to put that together?"

The adults got their food next, and once they'd settled down, everyone began to eat in silence. I wished Dad had put some music on.

"So," Aunt Cathy said after a few minutes, "it's one of my favorite times of the year! Let's all go around the table and say what we're thankful for."

My mom clapped rapidly. "Yes! Good idea, Cathy. Who wants to go first?"

"I'll go," Oli said instantly. "I'm so thankful to be here with my family, eating this delicious food, and I feel so blessed to be surrounded by such loving people. I pray for all of you every day, and I know God is smiling down on us tonight."

"Aw!" my mom said, filling up her champagne glass. "You're so sweet, little Oliver!" He blushed, and she looked at Jack, who was seated next to him. "Your turn, honey!"

He pursed his lips and thought for a few seconds. "I'm also thankful for my family"—his eyes flashed to me for a split second—"and I'm glad we're here together."

My mom blinked for a few seconds and finally said, "Aw, that was sweet too. Gillie?"

Gillie was seated at the head of the kids' table, my brother and sister on either side of her, and she looked like she wanted to squash all of us with a giant rolled-up magazine.

"I'm thankful for best friends, and for R.G."—she began to giggle furiously, but no one else reacted— "oh, sorry, inside joke, *I guess*. And, uh, I guess my family, too."

It was technically Ella's turn next, but unless she was especially grateful for explosions of mashed potatoes and peas, it didn't look like we were going to get anything substantial out of her.

"Baylor?" Grandpa By said.

"Right," I said, looking around the table at everyone

watching me. "Well, I'd hate to sound unoriginal, but I'm also thankful for all of my family, including everyone here tonight, and I know I'm sort of a weirdo with what I can do and everything, but . . . yeah, I'm also thankful I have the opportunity to help so many people all the time. It's really nice to pass on these healing messages to people who, whether or not they realize it, need some help."

Most of the adults looked at me with tears shimmering in their eyes. Aunt Hilda and Uncle Horty, however, seemed quite unmoved.

"Oh!" Kristina said excitedly. "My turn!"

"Glenn, you're next." My mom sniffled.

"Actually," I interjected, "Kristina would like to say something."

Everyone was silent as I looked directly to my left and nodded to Kristina to continue. She seemed stumped for a moment. "I . . . I *hate* that you're the one who's saying my words for them to hear," she said. "It's going to come out all wrong."

"She's saying she's really grateful to have a loving, understanding brother like myself to pass along her messages to you all," I said. "Aw, Kristina, stop! That's too nice."

"Demon dung," she said, rubbing her temples. "Just tell them I'm thankful I have the opportunity to be their guardian angel, and that I look forward to meeting them all one day—but not too soon."

I repeated her words verbatim, and all the adults had tears streaming down their cheeks. Everyone, that is, except Uncle Horty and Aunt Hilda. I'd totally been right about them converging into a hurricane of unpleasantness. It was a category five ice storm coming from them.

No one else seemed to notice, though, as they popped open another bottle of champagne and refilled their glasses.

"Well," Uncle Glenn said, "it's been truly beautiful to see my children"—and he choked up for a second as he turned to glance at my mom—"and my sister's children . . . express themselves so eloquently this evening. . . ." *Sniff*. "And I feel so lucky and blessed to be a part of such a wonderful family. We don't get to spend nearly enough time together, and I dearly treasure moments like these."

"Oh, *cheers!*" my mom said, raising her glass across the table from him. "I don't even have to go, honestly. Glenn took every single word right out of my mouth." She clanged her glass against her brother's and took a deep sip.

Grandma Renee was next to go, and she talked for a solid five minutes about her grandkids, dedicating nearly a minute to each of us. When she addressed me, though, she mentioned something odd.

"And Baylor, you're so gifted. So gifted. Sometimes I think back through all my decades on earth and I literally don't know anyone more gifted than you. But you carry a heavy burden. You have to deal with things other kids don't have to deal with, not until they're much older. And, I don't know, maybe you have to see way more than you'd like, too, whether it's through visions or dreams, and I just want you to know, even if you do already know this, that people do learn, and they do change. They do their best with what they have at the time."

She smiled at me, except it looked much more like a frown. A bucket of ice had splashed through my guts at her mention of dreams. There was no way for her to know I could peer into dreams, but part of me felt both guilty and suspicious—guilty because my intrusion into her dream was clearly weighing on her, but suspicious because . . . well, she seemed to know too much. Could she have really known I entered into her dreams? No. There was no way. She couldn't know. Aiden couldn't know. Bobby definitely couldn't know. No one could know. It was beyond all reason.

Aunt Hilda was next.

"I'm grateful for a family who knows what family is all about." She spoke more loudly than usual and looked at my mom and Glenn for a bit as she spoke. Then she focused her attention on Uncle Horty. "Most of us, anyway."

She tilted her glass in his direction and took a sip. An icy chill passed between them.

I looked at Gillie and raised my eyebrows, but she looked just as confused.

My dad was at the other head of the table, directly across from Gillie.

"Not sure I have much new ground to cover," he said quickly. "Family, friends, happiness, the usual sort of stuff. Cheers to all of us being together." He raised his glass of champagne and took a swig.

Uncle Horty was next. My dad was nervously chewing on his bottom lip as though it were the most scrumptious part of the feast.

"I'm thankful," he said very slowly, "to have been blessed with such a loving family. My sweet daughter, her caring husband, my wonderful grandkids. You've got to be some of the best people I've ever met." Aunt Cathy's shoulders slumped back, a light smile on her face, visibly relieved.

"Truly," he continued, "it's an honor to know such a forward-thinking group of people who're able to look beyond the familial problems of the past and focus on the good."

My dad's jaw clenched, and Uncle Glenn glanced at Uncle Horty with a dangerous look in his eyes.

"There are no problems here, Horty," Grandma Renee said with forced sweetness. "Not real ones, anyway."

"Please, Renee," he said, holding his hand up in front of her face. "I just have to say it. I may have said other things in the past, but I've changed. I think it's great you accept Baylor so outright and unconditionally. Kudos to you all." He raised his glass and took a sip.

The icy chill that initially passed between Horty and Hilda had taken the opportunity to slither down my throat and freeze my insides.

My dad was the one to speak first. "Horty, I swear to God," he said, pointing his finger at his face, nearly jabbing his eye, "if you say one more word, I'm going to . . ." He stopped talking, chewing his lips violently, holding his glass right against his lips.

"You know I don't say this from a mean-spirited place!" he said, his voice light, laughter brimming. "But we can all admit it's extremely unnatural."

My heart pounded in my chest. I looked at Kristina, whose mouth was wide open as she gaped back at me.

"He's just being a jerk," she said. "Don't listen to him."

"Dad, you promised me you wouldn't say any-thing," Aunt Cathy whispered furiously.

"The boy's a teenager," he said, taking another quick sip, "and he's on national news, for Pete's sake! You think I'm the only one out there saying this? We can't have a real discussion about it? Please. I'm sure he's heard this from a thousand people."

"No," I said, my voice low and shaky. "I actually haven't."

Was this why my dad had such a problem with him? Because he was so openly critical of my gift? But Aunt Hilda wasn't exactly my biggest fan, either. Granted, she was never this rude about it, but she'd had her moments.

"Believe me, Baylor, it's going to happen," he said. "Many people think the same way I do. You're unnat-ural, Baylor. You're a freak."

"Horty!" my mom growled, her eyes lethal. "His gift might be a bit unusual, but Baylor is perfect just the way he is."

He shrugged. "Whatever helps you sleep at night, dear."

"That's enough," Uncle Glenn said forcefully. Aunt Cathy sipped her champagne, looking dejected.

"You all know I'm right," he said, sipping slowly. "I can see it in your eyes whenever the boy talks about the *other side.*" He eyed Jack. "And who knows what else will come next." Jack, who'd been trying to escape the conversation by willing himself to shrink to the size of a G.I. Joe and live forever on his plate among the mountains of mashed potatoes and rivers of gravy, looked startled.

Uncle Horty smiled strangely at Aunt Hilda.

"I think she agrees with me."

"My own issues with Baylor aside," she said coldly, "I'd never say what you've said about him. Or the rest of them."

"Who?" I said. "What did he say?"

"Them!" he said, motioning lazily to Jack and Ella. "They should never have been born!" He turned back to my parents. "It's that simple. God knows what else you two are capable of bringing into this world. It's only a matter of time before we see what monsters they'll become."

15

TV stardom isn't all it's cracked up to be.

JACK LOOKED ON IN HORROR, BUT ELLA continued to slap her potatoes and peas in pure baby bliss, much to my jealousy.

"Jack and Ella are normal," I said, wishing I could erase this moment from Jack's mind.

"Ah, so you admit you're not normal," Uncle Horty said pointedly, his rectangular head leaning in.

"No, that's not what I meant at all," I said.

"Horty," my dad said, gripping the edge of the table, "I'm going to ask—"

"You're not about to give me another black eye, are

you, Dougy?" Horty asked. "We wouldn't want to
open that can of worms again, would we?"

My dad swallowed hard, his face burning bright red. Before he could respond, though, Mom stood up.

"Enough," she growled, wobbling slightly as she put her arms on the kitchen table and leaned forward to Horty, the light from the candles dancing around her face. "Enough! I can't believe it's Thanksgiving dinner at my house"—she pounded her chest—"and I have to sit here and listen to you! You, of all people! I didn't even want you here. My poor friend Karen and her son are sitting alone in their house right now eating pizza, and you're sitting here, ungrateful, smug, with your family, in *my house*, insulting *my children*?" She shook her head, kicking off her shoes. "No. Nope. That is not how this going to go. Glenn, grab him."

Horty had been listening to her speech with an odd triumphant smirk, but his face suddenly fell in confusion as Glenn, unsure of what his sister meant, grabbed Horty by his arm and looked helplessly at his sister.

"Everyone, grab a piece of him, please," she sang. "The more the merrier." Dad grabbed his other arm, Grandpa By took hold of the back of his neck, and even Grandma Renee snuck in and pinched his shirt collar. He started to protest—"You can't be serious?

What are you doing?"—but no one listened.

"Outside," she said, grabbing Horty's plate and marching barefoot down the hall. "Follow me. Baylor, grab their car keys from the counter."

I ran to the kitchen to find the keys and caught up with them as they led him out the front door, down the driveway, and back to the car he had such difficulties freeing himself from earlier. Mom took the keys, unlocked the car, and opened the back door.

"What are you doing to him?" asked Gillie. I couldn't tell whether she was concerned or having the time of her life. Oli stood next to her, looking like he was about to cry but smart enough to know it was not the time to protest.

"Inside," Mom said, glaring at Horty. "Buckle him up in the middle seat." Her feet must have been freezing on the pavement, but she stood there defiantly as my dad and Glenn settled him inside the car.

"This is wildly immature," he yelled helplessly as the men finished up. "You're just going to leave me here?"

Mom stuck her torso in the driver's seat, turned on the ignition, and said, "I'll get the heat going. Wouldn't want you to freeze to death." Then she paused. "Well, I'm sure Cathy wouldn't, at least."

"You can't be serious."

"I've never been more serious about anything in my life," she said viciously as she dropped the plate of food onto his lap. "And if you so much as look at one of my children again—you know, the ones who should've never been born—I will personally be the one to make you wish *you'd* never been born."

Then she slammed the car door in his face and laughed gleefully.

"*Wow*," Charlie gushed from behind me. "What a woman."

Grandpa By patted Mom on the back and guided her toward the house, singing her praises all the while. "It was a little extreme, sure, I'll give you that, but you're a true O'Brien, Connie. I gotta ask, you sure you want to stick with that Bosco nonsense still? Honestly, it makes a lot more sense for you to be an O'Brien, with you, and the anger, and the defending the family, and the showing-whose-boss, it's all very O'Brien."

Aunt Cathy, lagging behind, said, "We can't really leave him out there, Glenn."

"He's fine," Uncle Glenn said. "The heat's on, he's got food, and we get to relax for a bit. Everyone wins."

Back inside, Mom was on the phone. "If you don't come right now, I will come get you and force you in the car. I just forced one person into a car, and I'm not afraid to do it again. . . . I don't care! Bring the pizza! Who really likes turkey anyway?"

And five minutes later, Mrs. Kirkwood and Aiden showed up, each carrying their own small pizza box.

"Our contribution to the feast!" Mrs. Kirkwood said as they entered the kitchen.

"You know there's an old man yelling in the car, right?" Aiden whispered to me.

I nodded. "Don't ever mess with my mom."

Mom gave her a big hug as Dad got another chair for Aiden to sit at the kids' table. We all took our places, Mrs. Kirkwood in Horty's old spot and Aiden next to me.

"Yes," Mom said suddenly as the adults passed around the champagne to top off their glasses, "I may have just put an elderly man in time out, and that's something I'm really going to think about for a while, but he deserved it. And *we* deserved it, too, because now I'm finally with my family"—she looked around the table, beaming at everyone, but lingering on Mrs. Kirkwood and Aiden—"and the only charity case is outside, stuck in the middle seat of a car."

After dinner, once everyone had eaten seconds and thirds (Aiden), we'd plopped onto the couches and waited until our stomachs had enough room for some pie. Gillie had once again taken control of the TV and was flipping aimlessly from channel to channel.

"Should we think about letting my dad back in?" Aunt Cathy asked. "It's been a couple hours. I bet he'd apologize."

Mom scoffed. "Cathy, I love you, but that man is not stepping foot inside this house again. There's a hotel downtown he can check into if there's any room. Otherwise, I hope he finds that backseat comfortable."

Aunt Cathy squirmed a little, but Uncle Glenn put his hand on her leg and shook his head.

"Wait, what was that?" he said suddenly. "Gillie, go back."

Gillie flipped to the previous channel, and once again, my face was plastered on the screen. Except this time, it was a video rather than a picture.

"*. . . exclusive video uploaded earlier today showing Baylor Bosco, the self-proclaimed thirteen-year-old medium who's been making a lot of appearances in the news these days, channeling spirits . . .*"

In the video I was looking around, my face fraught with concern, reacting to things no normal person could see or hear. And I was wearing the same sweatshirt I'd been wearing all day. And the background was the family room, where we were sitting now.

All the adults turned my way, confused, but Kristina, who'd shot over from chatting with the colonel and Charlie in the kitchen, turned to gawk at Gillie.

"Is that . . . ?" Grandma Renee said. "Is that from today?"

Mom looked from the TV to me to Gillie. Gillie was gaping at the TV, her mouth wide open. She turned to me, her expression fighting between horrified and thrilled, a small smile on her mouth.

"Oh my God!" she said, covering her mouth, laughing in disbelief. "That's the video from earlier."

"You were recording me?" I asked.

"I wanted to show my friend Erin what you look like when you're channeling ghosts."

"Oh," I said meekly, turning back to the TV.

"*. . . already racked up twenty thousand views in less than three hours . . .*"

Talk about a slow news day. I didn't know what to say, but luckily I didn't have to say anything.

"Gillie," Grandma Renee said, her voice stern and unfamiliar, "how could you do that to your cousin?"

Uncle Glenn was nearly foaming at the mouth and kept saying, "You . . . you did that?" over and over.

Aunt Cathy, already on edge thanks to everything that had happened with her dad, was livid. She stood up, gripped Gillie's arm, and yanked her away to the office, where she screamed at her for twenty minutes. Our house was an old New England house, with hardwood floors throughout and very open vents, which meant we could hear every single word.

"How could you do this to your cousin? You've betrayed his trust, my trust, your father's trust, your aunt's and uncle's trust. And might I remind you you're spending Thanksgiving in their *house*, where we are right now?"

"But I didn't post it, Mom!" Gillie said, clearly crying. "I sent the video to Erin. She's the one who did it."

"Do you seriously think I care?" Aunt Cathy hissed, her voice positively lethal. "Do you think I give a single hoot about the logistics of how your silly little video got posted? You recorded it, Gillie, so you take responsibility for it. This is the last thing this family needed right now. You are grounded, young lady, for as long as I care to think about. You're lucky home-coming already happened, because you'd be home for that, and you can forget about the winter formal."

"But Jake already asked me to go! And we already have the limo at Lauren's house!"

"Jake's going to be awfully lonely, I guess, and you can pay me back for the cost of that limo, by the way."

"What? I don't have any money!"

"You know what? The other day, I saw the gas station was hiring a cashier. That seems like the perfect way to earn some money."

"What! No! You can't make me get a job! It's not even legal. You have to be fifteen."

There was a brief silence, where I could almost see Aunt Cathy mentally tossing around her options, and she finally said, "If that's true, then you're officially our new full-time snow shoveler. I'm canceling the service as soon as we get home!"

Yikes. That was brutal. I wanted to tell Aunt Cathy that I really didn't think the video was that bad. There had been much worse things done to me, some of them as recent as a couple hours ago, but deep down I knew it didn't matter. Gillie's timing couldn't have been worse, and she was going to pay the price.

Aiden and his mom chose that moment to slip out.

"Are we hanging out tomorrow?" he asked as I walked them to the door.

"Um, let's play it by ear," I said. "It's been a really weird day. I need to make sure everything's cool here first. Sorry you had to see that."

"Are you kidding?" he exclaimed. "It was way more entertaining than hanging out with just Mom."

They awkwardly ignored Uncle Horty's shouts and pleas for liberation from the middle seat and drove away.

"Oh no," Kristina said sadly as she watched them drive away, "he left without getting any pie."

As I walked back to the family room, Gillie ran from the office to my room upstairs. Aunt Cathy, her face flushed and her eyes wet, shook her head as she saw me. "This has been the worst Thanksgiving ever."

That night Aunt Cathy collected Horty's stuff from Jack's room and drove him to a hotel. She was going to rent a car and drive him back in the morning; Uncle Glenn, Gillie, and Oli would stay for another day to visit with everyone.

"That was one for the books, wasn't it?" Grandpa By said to Grandma Renee as they headed out the door with Aunt Hilda. "Very exciting. Too much excitement, maybe, for the bad heart."

"Bad heart?" I said, my voice panicky. "What? Are you sick?"

Grandma rolled her eyes. "He's fine. He's a hypochondriac."

"Don't listen to her, Baylor," he said, grabbing my shoulders to huddle with me. "We O'Briens have a history of heart disease. You're never too young to start taking care of yourself, you got that? Go for the broccoli instead of the cake. Put down the red meats and pick up the celery. Say sayonara to salt and say 'hey there, cutie' to Cuties—you know, those weird little oranges?"

"How much champagne have you had?" Grandma asked him.

"Probably a whole bottle," he said, hiccupping out the door.

She shook her head and followed him out.

"Baylor," Aunt Hilda said quietly. "I may not like your gift"—she reached up and touched my cheek—"but you're not so bad." Then she hobbled after them. "Don't forget about the old broad!" she called out.

Gillie had moved into Jack's room, and Jack didn't even protest because he was still excited to have a slumber party with me and Oli—well, mainly Oli.

"Baylor," Oli said as I turned out the lights, "you don't, like, see ghosts in your sleep, right?"

I looked at Jack and wondered how truthful to be. "I do sometimes, yeah, but that doesn't mean you're going to see any. I'm the only one unlucky enough to see ghosts all the time."

"Hey!" Kristina said.

"Just kidding," I mumbled.

"I know what you're trying to do," she said, "but it's still sort of hurtful."

I rolled my eyes. "Good night," I said, to both her and the boys.

"Good night?" Oli said. "Aren't we gonna stay up and tell stories and . . ."

But, sadly for Oli, I'd already drifted off to sleep.

I don't know whether I actually felt closer to Archie and Helena than ever before, or if I was just pretty stressed from seeing myself on national TV twice in a day, but when I fell asleep, I somehow wound up right on Loved Ones' Lane and headed straight for the edge of the lane to the vast ocean below. The stars overhead twinkled brighter than I'd ever seen them, like they were trying to convey an urgent message.

I didn't even wait to see if I could spot them in the distance—I channeled my inner cliff jumper and threw myself off the edge, swan-diving into the ocean. As my arms cut through the water, my legs pumping just as fast, I couldn't help but think I was breaking some kind of Olympic record. Of course, I wasn't actually swimming and didn't feel tired, but still, it had to require *some* kind of energy.

I arrived at the boat after a few minutes and crawled up the slippery edge with relative ease. Archie and Helena were lying on their backs, their faces glowing an eerie blue-white from the moon. The light cast uneven shadows across their faces; the bags below

Helena's eyes were cavernous, while her skin, now papery and peeling, seemed to have aged fifty years. The water in the bottle strapped to Archie's wrist was nearly gone; the strap had chafed against his skin, rubbing it raw and leaving a bloody pink handcuff that streaked violently against his skin.

"I'm here again, Archie," I said as I settled on the boat between them. "Are you okay?"

"What about me?" Helena asked, her voice raspy and harsh. She turned her head my direction, her eyes doing their best to focus on me. They settled on a focal point somewhere above my left shoulder.

"You can see me?" I asked, shocked. "I thought this was Archie's dream."

"Does it matter whose dream it is?" she asked, a hint of lightness in her voice. "That's no excuse for bad manners."

I didn't know whether to laugh or tell her this was no time for jokes. They'd been stranded on a boat for days, with seemingly no chance of rescue in sight. Then again, all things considered, in the face of such a dire situation, maybe now was the perfect time for some jokes.

"Now, now, Helena," Archie croaked, his deep voice even raspier than hers, like his vocal cords had turned into sandpaper. "That's no way to treat our guests. Especially the ones who aren't trying to eat us."

"That shark was only acting on his instincts," she said. "If we could talk Sharkese, I think we'd have made decent friends."

They each chuckled lightly as I sat there, unable to believe they weren't panicking.

"Baylor, you look like you've seen a ghost," Archie said, his sundried, cracked lips forming a thin smile on his face.

"That's an understatement," I said under my breath. "I know this is probably a dumb question, but do you two have any idea where you are right now? Have you seen any kind of landmark or something I could tell the authorities to help them find you?"

Archie's delirious expression slowly shifted, and his eyes suddenly looked sharp and alert. "What are you?"

"I'm a medium, Archie, and somehow I can talk to you and Helena. Normally I can only talk to dead people, but somehow I can communicate with you two. Unless . . ." I thought of Kristina talking about the Lost Souls and I gulped. "Unless you *are* dead? In which case, maybe I could help you?"

"They're not dead," came a voice from behind me. I jumped in surprise and wound up sliding off the boat, splashing awkwardly into the water. When I resurfaced, I saw Kristina floating above me, her form emanating blue energy. For a second, before I could wipe the water from my eyes, her blurry image looked powerful and majestic, like an angel had materialized before us.

"Kristina!" I said. "What are you doing here?"

"I needed to come assess the situation for myself," she said, her voice stoic.

"Is that an angel?" Helena croaked.

"Must be," Archie said. "She's too pretty to be human."

Kristina looked at Archie, her expression a mixture of sweet and sad.

"Gross," I said. "That's my sister." I pulled myself back onto the boat while Archie shrugged.

"Guess we know who got the looks in the family," he said.

"I'm trying to help you, you know," I said.

He looked left and right and frowned. "Well, we're still in the middle of the ocean, but I'm sure you're trying your hardest."

Kristina snickered, and Archie looked at her affectionately. "You really are an angel, aren't you? I feel safe looking at you."

Kristina didn't respond like I thought she would.

I thought she'd be gross and flirty with Archie, but instead she just sort of looked sadly at him.

"We'll do our best to help you, Archie," she said. "And you too, Helena."

"Can you check on our families too?" Helena asked. She sounded choked up and her eyes were sad, but she was too dehydrated to make tears. "I'm so worried about my parents. My mom must be losing her mind."

"I got in touch with them after I talked to Archie last time," I said. "I'm . . . uh, I'm not sure they believed me."

"It was my mom's birthday a couple days ago. At least I think it was a couple days ago. I feel like we've been here for weeks."

"It's Thursday night, and you've been missing since last Friday."

"Oh," she said, dazed. "Wow. Her birthday was Sunday. She loves elephants, you know. I got her an elephant statue made out of sea glass as a present." Her lip quivered. "I hope I get to give it to her." She swallowed hard.

My eyebrows shot up. "Where's the present, Helena? Where'd you put it?"

"It's in the bottom drawer of my nightstand, underneath some tank tops."

"That's it," I said, shooting a fervent glance at Kristina. "That's how I can get them to believe me!"

She nodded. "Maybe get something from Archie, too?"

"Archie, what's something I can use as proof that you're alive? Something no one would really know, especially not some random kid from New Hampshire?"

"Hmm," he thought, stroking his chin. "What's something good?" A large wave hit the boat then, rocking us back and forth. His hands grasped the edge of the boat and he clenched his face. "If I slip off, I'm not sure I'll be able to get back on," he said, suddenly serious for the first time.

"Don't say that, Archie," Helena said, terrified. "Don't even joke about that."

"Sorry," he said quietly. "I won't slip off. I'm too scared our shark friend will return."

"I'm learning Sharkese as fast as I can, Archie," Helena said. "I'll tell him you don't taste very good, that he'd be wasting his time on you."

"That's very considerate of you," Archie said with mock sincerity. "It's an obvious lie if you ask me, but I appreciate it nonetheless."

"Back to business," I said, worried another wave would come crashing over the boat and knock me back to Loved Ones' Lane with nothing to show for Archie. "Give me anything, Archie."

"I'm wearing my favorite board shorts," he said, pointing to his bathing suit. They were dark red with large graphic Hawaiian flowers on the sides. "My mom got them for me on a cruise ship."

"So random," I said. "Perfect."

"Those are so old and ugly," Helena said. "You really need a new pair."

"I'll just head to the mall now," Archie said. "Want to come with?"

"Sure," Helena said. "I could really use some toothpaste. And a burger."

"Great, we'll stop at the Toothpaste and Burger Store after I get my swimsuit."

"My favorite store," Helena said, giggling. "So many kinds of toothpastes and burgers."

"They go hand in hand," Archie said, laughing. "Who'd have thought it?"

I truly couldn't believe it. They'd been stranded for nearly a week, but they were still able to laugh with each other. If I were stranded on a boat with Aiden for a week, I'm not sure I would have been so friendly with him. In fact, I'm pretty sure I would have already turned into a cannibal by that point.

"You two really are best friends, aren't you?"

Kristina asked, still floating above us like some kind of massive blue firefly.

Helena smiled up at the moon and nodded. "The best."

"Friends till the oceans dry up," Archie said.

"Till the sun turns cold."

"Till Greek food stops being so delicious."

"Oh, you know the way straight to my heart, Archie Perceval."

He shrugged. "What can I say? It's true."

I smiled at them, but out of the corner of my eye I saw Kristina's expression shift. I had never seen her look more concerned.

"Time to go," I said, looking at her pointedly. "Archie, Helena, I'll be back soon. Stay safe, okay?"

"We'll be here," Archie said dryly.

I reached up for Kristina's hand, and she took hold, lifting me up out of the ocean and back to Loved Ones' Lane.

"Now *that's* cool," Archie shouted from a hundred feet below.

Once we were back on the lane, I asked her why she'd looked so serious back there.

"I looked as serious as you did," she said.

"No," I said, "because I was so confused the entire time by how they were acting. I would be panicking in their situation, but they seem to be in such good spirits. You, however, looked like you could see a tsunami a mile away heading straight for them."

She shook her head. "I'm just worried about the two kids stranded miles and miles away from shore. That's all."

"Well, maybe now we'll be able to help them!"

She shook her head again. "You got information about a birthday present and a swimsuit. That'll comfort the parents, sure, but Baylor, that's not going to help anyone find them."

I shook my head. "Yes, it will. It'll help encourage them to ramp up the search efforts."

She smiled weakly. "I hope you're right."

TIP

16

Don't be afraid to rip up your soul.

I WOKE UP, TIPTOED OVER JACK AND OLI, and snuck into the bathroom to leave another message on the hotline.

"Hi, this is Baylor Bosco again. I have new information. If someone could please call me back, I'd appreciate it." I left my number again and hung up.

"Smooth," Kristina said. "I like the air of mystery around the message."

"I don't want to give the news or Carla Clunders any ammunition."

"That . . . or you don't want the *Baylievers* to have any new fodder to comment on."

I blushed. "That didn't cross my mind at all."

"Sure it didn't," she said.

"Anyway," I said, "I don't know what to do. How can I help them?"

She shook her head. "I'm not sure you can."

"Then why am I seeing them? There's got to be something I can do."

She didn't say anything, and I got the feeling again that she knew something she wasn't telling me. I tilted my head and narrowed my eyes. "What is it?"

"Nothing," she said quickly.

"Can't you go ask your spirit guides or something?"

She smiled meekly. "Do you really think I haven't discussed this thoroughly with them?"

"Well? What did they say?"

"They wouldn't tell me anything useful," she said. "I'm just as in the dark as you are."

"You're my connection to the other side, Kristina," I said, feeling irritated. "If you can't tell me anything useful, then . . ."

"Then what?" she said sharply. "What's the point of my entire existence? Thanks a lot, Baylor."

"That's not what I was going to say."

"Then what were you going to say? Finish that sentence."

"If you can't tell me anything useful, then . . . I don't know . . . then we're not going to be able to help Archie and Helena."

She shook her head. "Well, in that case, maybe you should focus more on *your* side of things."

Maybe she was right. I had some resources on my side; perhaps it was time to use them.

Since I was up so early, I texted my friends to figure out plans for the day. To my surprise, they were up too. We decided to meet downtown at two o'clock (after scarfing down leftover turkey sandwiches at home, of course).

The morning passed by slowly. The adults weren't functioning at 100 percent, a consequence of last night's champagne and wine. Everyone grazed on leftovers and camped out in front of the TV for most of the morning.

Once it was nearly one o'clock, I announced that I was meeting up with friends downtown in case anyone wanted to join.

"Well, that sounds fun," Uncle Glenn said. "We should all go." To my astonishment, everyone nodded in agreement, and they got up to get ready. Gillie was the lone holdout, and she sat on the couch, staring gloomily at the TV.

"Not coming?" I asked.

She shrugged. "Whatever."

"All righty then," I said, getting up just to move away from her.

"You ruined my life, you know," she said.

I turned slowly to face her. "Excuse me?"

"It's all your fault. If you weren't such a freak, I wouldn't be grounded in the first place."

I had felt sorry for her up until five seconds ago. Now I was just furious.

"You've got a lot of nerve trying to blame any of this on me," I said. "You're the one who recorded me in the first place."

She glared at me. "Grandpa Horty was right about you. You should never have been born."

I didn't know what to say, but before I could think of anything, Kristina tuned me in to show me her aura. Auras are the outward reflections of people's souls, and Gillie's was a deep blood red. She was furious.

"Just walk away, Baylor," Kristina said. "It's her anger talking. Nothing positive will come of this."

I glared back at Gillie for another second, but walked away. Kristina was right—it wasn't worth engaging her. I was still mad, though. How dare she use Horty's words as a weapon against me? Maybe Uncle Glenn was right—maybe she did need a good exorcism.

We loaded into the cars and headed downtown. Aiden and J were already in the square; Bobby was late because he had eaten too much turkey and was moving slow. I waved to them as we circled around to find a spot on one of the side streets.

"What's up, guys?" I said as my family swarmed around them a few minutes later. I introduced them to my uncle and cousins, and everyone said hello except Gillie, who sneered unpleasantly the entire time.

"Where shall we go first?" Uncle Glenn asked.

"I need to do some, uh, research for a bit, but I'll meet up with you guys later."

"Research?" Mom asked. I couldn't see her eyes behind her dark sunglasses, but I knew she'd be looking at me suspiciously. "Lead the way, Baylor. You're not going anywhere without us."

My mouth dropped open while Kristina laughed loudly. "This should be fun."

"You guys will think it's boring," I said. "Don't worry about me."

"Baylor, sometimes I think you forget you're only

thirteen," Mom said. "We're sticking together. Lead the way."

I sighed. "Fine." I spun around and marched in the direction of Madame Nadirah's Mystic Shoppe.

The bell rang when I opened the door, and Madame Nadirah appeared from the back room and said, in her faux breathy voice, "Welcome to Madame Nadirah's Mystic Shoppe!" Then she noticed it was me and chuckled. "Baylor Bosco, my favorite customer." She swept me into a hug as my mom lifted her sunglasses and surveyed the scene in surprise.

"You two know each other?"

"Of course!" Madame Nadirah said, laughing. "I helped Baylor cross into another dimension a few weeks ago to find his missing sister." My eyebrows shot up nearly as fast as my mom's.

"*Anyway,*" I said sharply, glaring at Madame Nadirah, "no need to bring up the past, it's all behind us, right? Onward!"

"Onward, indeed," she said, glancing at the crowd that had followed in behind me. "Is this your family?"

"And two friends," I said, motioning to J and Aiden, who were off admiring the huge display of candles, crystals, dream catchers, and essential oils.

"Oh my," she said hoarsely, seized by Gillie's

presence. "Girl, you are hurtin'!" She grabbed a small bottle of sage essential oil from the counter, rubbed some into her palms, and then placed her hands over Gillie's temples.

Gillie stood there in shock and said, "What do you think you're doing?"

"Breathe deeply, my girl," she said, inhaling and exhaling dramatically. "Breathe deeply. Let that anger out."

Gillie, to my surprise, listened to her instructions, and her shoulders slumped.

"Feel better?" Madame Nadirah asked.

"A little," Gillie said faintly.

"Mmhmm, yep, you do," she said. Then she turned to me. "You have a question for me."

It wasn't a question; she could sense I was there for a reason. Madame Nadirah wasn't a medium like me, but she was connected to the other side as an empath— her intuitive energy was as keen as a search dog's nose. And that's why I was here. I needed her help to figure out how I could save Archie and Helena.

I rushed forward, grabbed her arm, and led her away from where my mom could hear us. "I only have a minute before my mom is going to try to eavesdrop, and honestly, it might be less than a minute, so listen carefully. You know those two Florida kids who've gone missing? They've been all over the news? I somehow can talk to them while I'm dreaming. I have no idea how."

"Does that mean they're dead?" asked Madame Nadirah.

"I don't think so. It's weird. I think it has something to do with being lost in the ocean."

"What does that have anything to do with it?"

"It's too long to explain now. I'm trying to figure out a way to help them, but I don't know how. There's no way for me to pinpoint their exact location; all I can do is talk to them."

"So you're looking for a way to track them?"

"I guess."

"Some kind of metaphysical beacon," she said quietly, looking around her shop.

"A what?"

"If you're meeting them through dreams, the object needs to exist in multiple realms so that you can access it in both the conscious and unconscious states."

"Right," I said. She may as well have been speaking Chinese. "So whaddaya got?"

She shut her eyes and tapped her foot for a few seconds. "I have an idea, but I'm not sure whether it'll work."

"That's still better than the nothing I'm working with right now."

She nodded. "Well, it's not going to be easy for you, Baylor."

"Why?"

"You'll need to leave a piece of your soul with them."

"I knew it," Kristina said sotto voce.

Kristina seemed far too calm. I wasn't expecting Madame Nadirah to say that, and a horrible sense of panic spread through me.

"What? My *soul*? I'm not messing with my soul! Besides, wouldn't I have to kill someone else to break a piece of it off?"

"This isn't some He-Who-Must-Not-Be-Named black magic, Baylor," she said, raising her hand fast. I thought for a second she was going to slap me upside the head, but instead she imitated holding a wand and casting a spell. "What, you believe everything you read?"

"Well, I don't know! It's not like I'm in the habit of breaking off little pieces of my soul to use as some kind of otherworldly bread crumb trail."

"There's a first time for everything," she said, her smile glinting with mischief.

"So what's the proper way to do it?"

"It's not as bad as it sounds, Baylor," Kristina said calmly.

"Is your sister there?" Madame Nadirah said sharply, looking right at Kristina. Kristina looked startled.

"Can . . . can you see me?" Kristina asked, a note of excitement in her voice.

"Because I can feel her," Madame Nadirah said. She lifted her left arm and sliced through Kristina. "I've had the chills for the last few seconds, but only on the left side of my body. And you keep looking right *there*." She flourished her hand dramatically at Kristina.

"Yeah, Kristina's there," I said. "She just said breaking my soul up isn't as bad as it sounds, though I'm going to have to disagree with that one."

"People leave pieces of their soul lying around all the time," Madame Nadirah said. "Almost always by accident too. They don't know they're doing it, but they can feel it." She must have noticed how confused I looked because she sighed and shook her head fast, as if she were trying to shake the perfect example into place. "Ever love a place so much that you feel like you're one with it?"

I immediately thought of my dad's parents' house down in Ohio. Grandpa Bosco had died years ago, but Grandma Nora still lived there. I'd had so many happy memories and occasions at that house—warm, pink-sky summer evenings running around the yard catching fireflies in glass mason jars, ice-cream parties with my cousins, endless sleepovers and movie nights with buckets of popcorn filled with M&M's—that I could close my eyes and feel like I was there.

"There!" Madame Nadirah said excitedly. "Whatever you just thought of—you've left a piece of your soul there."

"My grandparents' house in Ohio?"

She nodded. "I'd bet my life savings, all ten bucks of it, that most people have left a piece of their soul at their grandparents' house. I'm assuming you had a lot of happy childhood memories there?"

"A ton!" I said, still feeling warm and fuzzy at the thought of those memories. "But I'm not sure I'd put two kids lost at sea on the same scale as all the memories at my grandparents' house. I don't want a piece of my soul floating around in the ocean. Who knows what could snatch onto it?"

"Baylor, a piece of a soul isn't going to tempt a demon," Kristina chimed in. "It'd want the whole thing."

"But still," I said, thinking of my soul, even though I wasn't entirely sure what it looked like. It tended to

change shapes a lot in my head. Today I imagined it
as a fiery white cage that surrounded my heart. "It's
my soul."

"But it's *their* lives at stake," Kristina said, sounding
more annoyed with every word. "You're thinking about
it too much. It'd be like thinking a fingernail clipping
was worth a million bucks. It's just not the case."

"I don't know what is going on between you two
right now," Madame Nadirah said, fanning herself,
"but, *oh*, there is some friction here."

I could see my mom watching us while pretend-
ing to look through a display of T-shirts. "Okay,
quickly—how do I leave a piece behind?"

"Well, this part is why I said it wouldn't be easy,"
she said. "You need to forge a strong emotional connection to the place. You know you've done it when
you can close your eyes and picture the place exactly
as it is. That's because you can glimpse it through
your soul—a part of you really is there."

"But . . ." I thought of the shiny capsized boat,
and the vast ocean with its rolling water as far as
the eye could see and the mind could imagine, and
two stranded kids struggling to stay alive. "But I
don't think I can. It's not exactly a place I want to
remember, and I'm not really sure I can fake something like that."

Madame Nadirah looked at me seriously. "You need to try real hard then, kid," she said. "Otherwise, you better hope one of those planes spots them soon."

By that point, Mom had inched her way over so close that I had no choice but to introduce her to Madame Nadirah. After they shook hands, my mom said, "So what were you saying earlier about other dimensions . . . ?"

I shot Madame Nadirah a look and shook my head, but before I could say anything, my phone started ringing. It was a Florida number.

"I've got to take this!" I said, running outside. After the door shut, I picked up and said, "Hello? This is Baylor Bosco."

There was a brief silence, and then the voice on the other end said, in a thick accent, "And this is Helios Papadopoulos. I'm Helena's father."

Bingo.

"Thanks for calling me back, Mr. Papadopoulos."

"This is not easy for me to do, young man," he said, swallowing loudly. "But it's been a week, and"—his voice trembled—"I'm desperate for anything that could help us find our kids."

"They're still alive, Mr. Papadopoulos. I'm trying to figure out a way to find them, but I know this much—they're alive and they're okay. They look like they've been sitting out in the sun for a long time with no food, but they're in decent spirits at least."

There was another long pause. "How am I supposed to believe you? Anyone could tell me something like this."

"Helena mentioned it was your wife's birthday last weekend."

"Yes," he said slowly, suspiciously. I heard an odd muffled noise on the line, too, but ignored it.

"She told me to tell you her present for your wife is in her nightstand, in the bottom drawer under some tank tops. It's an elephant figurine made out of sea glass."

I heard a screech and a crash on the line, and I pulled the phone away from my ear. "What was that?" I asked loudly. "Are you okay?"

"My apologies," he said, his voice deep and shaky. "I have you on speakerphone, and my wife knocked over her chair in her hurry to get to Helena's room."

"Oh," was all I could muster. I imagined my mom in Mrs. Papadopoulos's shoes, desperately looking for any piece of me that might serve as a clue, or a memory. It was just a couple days ago that I'd seen her crying on the news alongside Archie's mom, begging for anyone to help them.

A loud shriek pierced my eardrums from the phone, and I had to hold the phone away once more.

"It's here," a female voice cried out. "Just like he said. It was exactly where he said. It's real." She sobbed violently. "*He's* real."

I heard Mr. Papadopoulos swallow repeatedly, but I didn't say anything. I wanted to let them process in silence.

"Baylor," he said, "you must come help us. You're the first person who's been able to tell us . . . anything, actually. The police, the coast guard, they've all been looking, but this is the first solid evidence we have."

"Honestly, I wouldn't be a lot of help at the moment," I said. "I'm trying to come up with a plan, but I have no way to find them."

"Then you can relay messages for us. We can pay for your plane ticket, for your parents' plane ticket. Heck, we have friends with seaplanes who have been aiding in the search. We could have one of them come fetch you."

"Seriously, if I thought my presence would help, I'd already be down there," I said. "But for now, it wouldn't do anyone any good."

"Baylor, this is Dina," Mrs. Papadopoulos said loudly into the phone. Her accent was strong, and she had a deliberate way of speaking. "How did she look? How did my baby look? Is she okay?"

I hesitated. "She and Archie were joking with each other, but . . . they look really weak," I said. I thought of that wave hitting the boat, and Archie saying he wasn't sure he'd be able to crawl back up if he fell off. "I know it's obvious, but we need to find them really, really soon."

"Archie," she said, a hint of anger in her voice. "I will never forgive him for this. He wasn't supposed to take the boat out by himself. He betrayed his father's trust."

"He mentioned he made a mistake . . . ," I said, trying to think of what else he said about it. But that was the first time I had seen them, and a giant wave slapped me back to Loved Ones' Lane a second later.

"A mistake," she scoffed. "Willful rule-breaking, more like it. This was no mistake. He knew he didn't have permission, but he did it anyway, and he dragged Helena out to sea with him."

"I'm really sorry this is all happening," I said. "I hope knowing they're alive and okay is helpful."

There was a silence. "It's been a week. How much longer can they go without food, without fresh water?"

"They had some water," I said. "But it was running low."

Another moment passed in silence, and I said, "I'll call back with any news." I almost hung up, but before I did, I had to say it. "And I know you're mad at Archie, but if you could tell his family that I know he's wearing his favorite red bathing suit with the flowers that his mom got on a cruise, that might comfort them, too."

Yet another silence, but finally Mr. Papadopoulos said quietly, "We'll tell them."

I hung up and took a deep breath. That was horrible.

I walked back inside to see Aiden finishing up a purchase from Madame Nadirah. He stuffed a small bag into his pocket while J chatted merrily with her about the shop's wide variety of candles.

"I can't believe I've never been in here before! Your selection is so amazing and unique. This is going to make the perfect Christmas gift for my mom."

"Ready to go, everyone?" I asked.

Gillie had curled up into a ball on a leather armchair in the corner of the shop, her expression as pleasant as a car crash. "Finally," she muttered, untangling herself and heading for the door. "This place gives me the creeps. And I *reek* of sage."

"You might want to reapply before you go," Madame Nadirah called out as the door shut behind her. Then, quietly, she said, "Though I doubt even a long soak in a swimming pool of sage would do *her* any good."

TIP

17

Try not to ruin your brother's life.

WE STOPPED AT THE ICE-CREAM SHOP JUST off the main square and took over one of the long tables inside as everyone licked their scoops. Other families might have let the frigid weather scare them away from getting ice cream, but the Bosco family firmly believes there's never a wrong time for it.

"Well, that was an interesting shop," Uncle Glenn said as some of his green mint chocolate chip dripped down his mouth. "You go there a lot, Baylor?"

"Not really," I said, trying to maintain control of my scoop, chocolate with chocolate sprinkles. For

some reason my ice cream was melting way too fast.
"Madame Nadirah has helped me a lot in the last couple weeks, though."

"She sure has," my mom said, eyeing me over her chocolate-vanilla swirl. "We had a *fascinating* chat while you were on the phone."

Kristina was standing by the glass icebox, examining all the flavors. "Oh, right, I forgot to tell you. You are *so* busted. Madame Nadirah told Mom all about your little adventure to find me and how you saw Grandpa Bosco and everything."

"Great," I said under my breath.

"It smelled weird in there," Oli said. His ice cream was melting fast, too, and the blue-pink of the cotton candy scoop was pooling on his hand. "Like someone set Grandma's perfume on fire."

"That was the incense," J said. She'd gotten a scoop of vanilla in a cup, covered with rainbow sprinkles and chocolate syrup. "It's supposed to purify the energy in a room."

"Oh," Oli said. "I'm not sure that worked very well." He started to lick the neon puddle off his hand.

"You're so disgusting," Gillie said. She hadn't ordered anything, and she sat at the table observing us all as though she were a patron at the world's least entertaining zoo.

"Be nice to your brother," Uncle Glenn said, but then he looked at Oli. "But your sister's sort of right, son. Just use a napkin."

"I'm not going to waste perfectly good ice cream!" Oli said.

Aiden, sitting directly across from Oli, nodded in understanding as he licked his Rocky Road.

Bobby entered the shop at that moment, but he wasn't alone. Cam Nguyen followed a second later, accompanied by his little brother, Minh, and another of his and Jack's classmates, a kid named Adam Rosenberg. I recognized him because our moms worked on the PTA together.

"Hey, guys! I ran into Cam a few blocks away!" Bobby said excitedly, his entire year clearly made over the coincidence.

I glared at Cam, while Jack focused diligently on his chocolate chip cookie dough, avoiding the glances of his classmates. Cam half-heartedly waved my way and pushed the two boys toward the icebox.

I got up and Bobby swooped into my seat. "You didn't call 'five'!" he said. "My chair now!"

Gillie, who'd been staring at the wall miserably, had transformed, suddenly fixing her hair and running her fingers through it repeatedly as she eyed Bobby. My mom introduced Uncle Glenn and Oli to Bobby, giggled loudly and said, "Aunt Connie, stop! Let him try to guess it!"

I rolled my eyes. As much as I'd enjoy watching Gillie embarrass herself in front of our family and my friends, I had questions for Cam.

"Carla Clunders?" I said to him. "Seriously?"

"She found *me*, Baylor," he said, not making eye contact.

"How?"

"I don't know," he said. "She just showed up at my house and started asking me questions about you."

"And you willingly talked to the random lady who just showed up at your house?"

"Look, I was mad at you still, all right?"

"And then you commented on the post too? 'CamTheMan'? Just try to tell me that's not you."

His wide cheeks burned red. That was all the proof I needed.

"I didn't mean to scare Minh, Cam. It was an accident. But you chose to say nasty things about me to that woman, so I hope you feel good about that."

I was about to turn back to my table when he said, "Baylor, wait." He was still staring at the ice-cream flavors, but he clenched his teeth and said, "Look, I'm sorry, okay? I shouldn't have said anything."

I nodded. "Fine. Apology accepted. See you Monday."

I turned around to see Jack peeking at us, except he wasn't staring at me and Cam chatting. He was looking at Minh and Adam.

"Actually," I said, turning back around to Cam. "Can I ask for a favor? A show of goodwill to smooth everything over?"

Cam furrowed his brows, looking reluctant to hear anything I had to say.

I leaned in and whispered. "Could you convince your brother to come hang out at my house for a bit? Tonight, maybe? I think it'd be good for him to spend time with Jack. And then he could see I'm not so scary, either."

He looked at the boys and then back at me. "I'm supposed to be babysitting them all day."

"I'll do that for you!" I said. "No problem. You can go hang out with your friends and my dad will drop them off later tonight."

He was chewing on his tongue as he weighed his options. "I feel like Minh and Adam wouldn't love the idea . . . but then again, I do really want to see the new Spider-Man movie with the guys tonight."

"It'll be fine. In fact, they can come back to my house now, and you can have the rest of the day to yourself. They'll be in good hands. I promise your Spidey senses won't be tingling!"

He blinked at me awkwardly.

"Just . . . just forget I said that last part," I said.

He looked down at Minh and Adam and shrugged. "Hey, boys, listen up!"

He told them the plan, and the boys looked from Cam to me then back to Cam, terrified.

"I think I should call my mom," Adam said, clearly trying to get out of it. "I don't think she'd like this idea."

"Our moms do PTA together," I said to him. "I think she'll be totally okay with it, actually."

His eyes widened, but he didn't say anything else.

For all I knew about Minh—and it wasn't much, besides what Cam had said about the whole nightlight situation—he seemed to be okay with the news.

"We'll have fun with Jack," he said to Adam. He almost sounded excited. "Just . . . stay away from . . . you know . . ."

Seriously? What did they think I was going to do to them? Unleash a demon to gobble up their souls? Didn't they realize we were likely freaked out by the same types of things on the other side?

Cam paid for their ice cream, gave me his cell phone number in case I needed to get ahold of him, and headed out.

"Hey, Jack, your friends are going to come hang out this afternoon," I said.

Mom immediately perked up, looking at the boys in confusion. "What? They are?"

"Yeah, that kid who just left, Cam, he's in band with us, and his brother Minh is in Jack's class. And you know Adam because Mrs. Rosenberg does PTA with you."

"Hi, Minh," my mom said, "and hi, Adam. Do your parents know you're with us? I usually talk on the phone with another mom before a playdate."

Minh shrugged. "Cam was babysitting us and he said it was okay." They pulled up chairs next to Jack, who was smiling widely, and began chatting with him about some game involving zombie-fighting plants.

I thought Mom was going to say something else, but she took another look at Jack's smiling face and her expression softened. She shrugged at me just as nonchalantly as Minh had, and then resumed licking her ice cream.

Once everyone was done with their ice cream, we took another loop around the square. I kept my eye on Jack, Minh, and Adam, who were chatting merrily behind the group. I glanced at Kristina, feeling hopeful that I was in the process of undoing whatever harm we'd done to Jack's life.

"Have you ever seen him talk so much?" Kristina asked.

I shook my head. I'd loosened up recently and started communicating with Kristina more directly when I was around friends, but I didn't want to risk any of Jack's friends seeing me look at or talk to what they perceived as air.

"Smart thinking about keeping mum," she said. "Wouldn't want to scare them just as they're starting to warm up." Kristina couldn't read my thoughts, but sometimes we definitely operated on the same wavelength.

Meanwhile, Bobby was telling me, Aiden, and J a story about how one of his older cousins taught one of his younger cousins to say the phrase, "Don't quit your day job," and the little cousin went around for three straight hours answering everything single thing with, "Don't quit your day job."

"It was a nightmare," he said, his fingernails digging into his skull. "Over and over and over. 'What's your favorite color, Johnny.' *Pshh. Don't quit your day job.* 'Hey, Johnny, do you like the mashed potatoes?' *Uh, don't quit your day job.* 'Johnny loves that new Disney movie, don't you, Johnny?' *Psh, don't quit your DAY JOB, Mom.* 'My day job is taking care of you, Johnny Boy, I'd never quit that.' That one really stumped him."

"Ha. It could have been much worse, though," J said. "Think of all the other idiomatic expressions out there."

"The what now?" Bobby asked.

"Idiomatic expressions," J said. "They're basically sayings that only make sense to a group of people who speak the same language and share the same culture. So, if you literally translated 'it's raining cats and dogs' into Spanish, they'd look at you like you were crazy because it wouldn't make any sense."

"Oh," Bobby said, "well, it doesn't really make sense in English, either."

"Right," J said. "Why cats and dogs? And why always in that order? If you said 'it's raining dogs and cats,' most English speakers would question it."

"Oh," Aiden said, "or whenever someone says 'it's a piece of cake.' I've watched my mom bake cakes. It's not easy."

J nodded. "Exactly. They're just phrases that make sense to us because, as a culture, we've collectively accepted them. You could come up with a phrase, assign it any meaning, and as long as everyone was cool with it, that'd be an idiomatic expression."

"Interesting," Bobby said, the wheels in his head turning. "I could say anything . . ."

"The world is your oyster," J said with a wry smile.

"I don't know who chose oyster instead of something like a burrito, which, quite frankly, offers a better assortment of options than an oyster could ever pray to compete with, but whatever."

"Right," I said. "What does an oyster offer the world besides a glob of gross snot in a shell?"

"It's so true," Bobby said. "The world is your burrito. Think of all the different options! White or brown rice? Black or pinto beans? The meats! The salsas! The toppings!" His eyes widened dramatically. "You've blown my mind, Janet Franklin."

J's whole body shuddered. "Never call me Janet," she said. "I'm still trying to figure out why my parents thought that was a good choice for a child not born in the 1930s."

"I like your name," Aiden said. "It's . . . sweet."

Bobby, J, and I looked at him for a loaded moment before we burst into laughter.

"Oh, Aiden, you're as cute as a button," Bobby said.

"As sweet as apple pie," J said.

"As cool as the other side of the pillow," I said.

We laughed as his cheeks burned nearly to the color of his hair.

"I'm serious!" he said. "Don't laugh at me!"

"We're not laughing at you, Aiden," J said. "We're just joking."

"No," he said, his mouth taut and furious. "You're laughing at me just because I said I liked your name? *Har har. Another dumb thing said by dumb Aiden. Aiden's so stupid and worthless, let's make fun of him, har har.*" He glared at each of us. "I'm sick of it."

He marched away, aimlessly, not in the direction of his house, but at least away from us.

"Wow," Kristina said, and she flickered something in my head to tune into Aiden's aura. It was as red as a tomato, just like Gillie's had been earlier.

"Aiden," I called out. "Come back. We're sorry!"

Hands dug deep into his pockets, his shoulders slumped, he kept walking away.

"What happened?" my mom asked.

"I'm not sure," J said. Her eyebrows furrowed, her eyes sad under her bright green glasses. "We were just teasing him and he got really mad at us."

But I knew. I knew it right when he said the word *worthless*. Aiden's dream was stuck in his head, those harsh words thrashing around and stinging like a horde of angry wasps.

That night, I still had Aiden on my mind, but despite sending numerous text messages, I got nothing back.

"Still worried about Aiden?" my mom asked as

she sat with Uncle Glenn and my dad at the kitchen table, watching me stare at my phone.

"I'm not worried about him," I said quickly.

She chuckled lightly. "Right," she said. "That's not what I meant. I just meant are you still thinking about him leaving suddenly this afternoon?"

I sighed and looked at Kristina.

"I mean, the answer is clearly yes," she said, shrugging and throwing up her hands. "Who are you kidding?"

"Not helpful," I said to her under my breath. Turning to my parents and uncle, I said, "It's just, uh, a little concerning he hasn't texted me back. He's usually instantaneous."

"Just give it time," Uncle Glenn said. "These things happen."

I pursed my lips and nodded, thinking that might have been the least helpful advice I'd ever received. "I'm going upstairs." Before I headed up, though, I peeked on Jack, who was playing a board game with his friends and Oli.

I walked away and said aloud to Kristina, "Perfect."

Upstairs, Colonel Fleetwood and Uncle Charlie were waiting in my room.

"Have you two been here the whole time?" I asked.

"Don't ask," Colonel Fleetwood said, his voice pleasant yet prickled with terseness.

"I'm having the best time," said Uncle Charlie, who somehow looked dirtier, like he'd gone to roll in the mud with a pack of dogs. "It's been like talking to a fossil. He doesn't even know how to use a telephone."

"Really, Uncle Charlie?" I said. "Can you explain what the Internet is?"

He frowned. "The what now?"

I turned to Colonel Fleetwood. "Care to fill in the blanks?"

The colonel looked at me, momentarily confused for some reason. "I'd . . . I'd be happy to," he said.

Kristina looked at me with the same confused expression as the colonel.

"You just defended the colonel," she said, as much to herself as to me, seemingly dazed.

"Just calm down," I said. "Don't get used to it."

"It's kind of nice," she said. "Not having to worry about you making some dumb, rude comment to him. You should feel guilty about Aiden more often."

"That's not what's happening here."

"Sure," she said. "I believe you."

"Stop it."

"Stop what?"

"You're so annoying."

She smiled. "You're as sweet as a button," she said.

"You're hilarious," I said, "meanwhile, can we just discuss real quick how I have to casually shave off part of my soul the next time I see Archie and Helena?"

"You're thinking about it too much," she said. "I can guarantee you it's not ever going to happen if you try to force it."

"All I *can* do is try to force it!"

"It's like Madame Nadirah was saying—you need to become one with the setting."

"Which," I said, "is absurd. Become one with the gigantic body of water that's about to eat up two kids my age. How could I become one with that kind of awful setting? I'd have better luck trying to leave a piece of my soul in a Porta Potty at the pumpkin festival."

"Gross, Baylor," Kristina said, rolling her eyes. "Look, I'm not 100 percent sure how you're going to make it happen, but if you want to save their lives, you're going to have to figure it out."

"I need to light a candle," I said. The stress of the problem, combined with the Aiden situation, and even the Uncle Horty fiasco from the previous night, were all building up some seriously bad juju.

I lit the wick and circled myself with light, feeling a little better, but even when some of the bad energy cleared away, there seemed to be plenty more waiting in the wings. Carla Clunders. The Baylievers. Gillie's bad attitude. Jack's precarious friend situation.

I put my hands over my face and sighed. This was not the relaxing Thanksgiving break any of us had been hoping for.

The most immediate of the new problems was Jack. He was downstairs having fun, and that was all I could really ask for. Everything was going smoothly— the last thing I needed was for some ghostly situation to arise and scare the crap out of his friends.

"Er, is that normal 'round these parts?" Uncle Charlie asked.

Kristina looked off to the side somewhere, and her eyes grew wide. "Baylor, tune in," she said. "Tune in right now."

Once again, I hadn't even realized I was tuned out. Actually, I'd barely delivered any messages the past few days, ever since I got the amulet. Was this what it was like to live a semi-normal life? Thinking I could really get used to it, I tuned back in, and though normally there was never much activity at home, tonight was a whole different story.

On one side of my room, I had what looked like a wedding taking place, while on the other side, a Christmas party was in full swing.

"Kristina," I said calmly, "what's going on?"

"I think Minh and Adam are wreaking havoc on the Bosco ecosystem," she said, sounding genuinely surprised. "These people just appeared out of nowhere! I've never seen such raucous relatives!"

"We wouldn't have to appear so suddenly if Baylor would let us pass on messages once in a while!" said a gyrating older man.

"It's only been a week!" I said. "Forgive me for not being at your beck and call every moment of my life."

"You didn't have to shut us out completely," said a woman, one of Minh's relatives, who wore a Santa hat and was holding a star-shaped paper lantern.

"Why are you already celebrating Christmas? It's not even December."

"We started celebrating in September!" she said. "One month of Christmas isn't enough!"

"That makes no sense," I said. "Do you even have a message for me to pass on, or is this some kind of call for help from the other side?"

"You hit the nail on the head," called out one of Adam's uncles. "We've been putting requests in to Kristina and Colonel Fleetwood and the others to have you tune in, but since we all clearly were met with deaf ears, we decided to take things into our own hands."

"By throwing a Christmas party? That seems a bit extreme."

"Oh?" said the aunt with the paper lantern. "It worked, didn't it?"

"Well, you finally have my attention," I said dramatically. "What is it? What could possibly be so urgent that you felt the need stage an intervention with me?"

"It's not something specific from any of us," said one of the uncles. "It's a message for you from the Beyond."

"What are you talking about?" Kristina asked. "All messages from the Beyond go through me." A note of pride reverberated in her voice

"This doesn't concern you, Kristina," the uncle said, suddenly sharp. "You think you're some expert on the Beyond just because you're special? You don't know everything."

Kristina scowled, her body suddenly shimmering with blue energy.

"How dare you come into my family's house and talk to us like that! I can tell you've been dead for less than five years. You're just a baby ghost! You know *nothing*."

"We didn't come here to fight," said the paper lantern aunt, her hands spread open in a gesture of peace. "We were selected since our loved ones are here."

"Who selected you?" Kristina said.

"What matters now," she said, her voice ominous, "is that Baylor acts carefully."

"Who sent you?" Kristina said, her voice a growl, suddenly tense, her body illuminated in blue. Next to her, Uncle Charlie and Colonel Fleetwood's forms were lapping with the blue energy. I didn't know what was happening, but I promptly lit a candle. It hissed and burned brightly, seemingly spurred on by the extra energy in the room.

"The other side is bigger than you can imagine," the uncle said as his fellow dancers began to shimmer and flicker. I hadn't taken a good look at all the people till now, but the dancers and the party revelers suddenly slowed down, and it dawned on me that they all looked very similar. In fact, they looked identical, as if they were a set of decatuplets—ten men and ten women who just so happened to look exactly alike.

"Kristina?" I said quietly. "Are you seeing what I'm seeing?"

Before she could respond, the ghosts began to shoot around in a blur, like some kind of pinball machine gone wrong, and I took a step back, nearly dropping my candle in surprise. At first it looked like they were zooming at high speed around my room, but then I realized they were disappearing, each form melding itself into the one that'd been talking to us the entire time.

After just a few seconds, we were left with just the two figures staring back at us, each of them deadly serious, their eyes focused on me.

"A change is coming," the woman said

"And your soul is at stake," the man said. They both spoke with grave authority.

I held the candle, unsure of how to respond. "Could you . . . could you maybe elaborate a bit more?"

The woman shook her head. "Proceed with caution, Baylor, lest the evil of the other side find its way to you."

"I think it's time for *you* to *leave*," Kristina said, her entire body illuminated in blue flash of light. A shock wave of energy passed through me, and the flame from the candle in my hands sizzled as it mingled with the energy. It grew stronger, combining with the blue and forming a fiery barrier that wrapped itself around the spirits that had come to warn me. The lights flickered, and suddenly, Kristina ignited, a blast of energy jutting outward.

"Kristina!" I yelled, dropping the candle and covering my eyes.

She zoomed out my door, the spirits knocked off

their feet and dragged along like two dolls on a rope. I ran after them, Charlie and Fleetwood close behind, as the lights continued to flicker. The front door flew open, and Kristina hurled the spirits out into the dark, where they tumbled in violent circles before landing on their feet, shooting me one last pointed look, and disintegrating into the night in a shower of blue-and-white sparks.

"What just happened, Kristina?" I yelled. "Are you kidding me? Were they good? Were they evil? Were they something else? And what did their message mean?"

Kristina stood just outside the doorway, defiant, her shoulders back and sturdy.

Before she had a chance to answer, I felt eyes on me from the side, and I saw my parents, Uncle Glenn, Gillie, Oli, Jack, and his friends Minh and Adam all staring at me from the foyer.

There was a pregnant silence, during which clearly no one knew what to do, and then Jack's friends ran screaming out the door into the dark.

"Adam! Minh!" my mom called after them as they ran outside. "Where are you going?" She gave chase, doing her best to stop two very scared and very fast seven-year-olds from going too far on their own.

My dad was looking at me like I'd just grown

another head, surely debating how much the whole "unconditional love of a parent" thing really applied in situations like this one. I, on the other hand, was looking at Jack, feeling awful.

He was still clutching a stack of playing cards from their interrupted game of Crazy Eights, his eyes wide and wet.

"Jack," I said, shaking my head. "I'm so sorry. I don't know what just happened, honestly." He looked at me, confused, and then looked out the door through which his friends had just run, blinking several times.

"Jack?" I said.

A few more seconds passed, but then he took a gulp and smiled at me. "That's okay, Baylor," he said, his voice cheerful but thin. He glanced at the playing cards in his hands. "I had fun while it lasted." Then he offered a tepid smile once more and turned around to head back to the family room as cards fluttered to the floor from his limp hand.

"My heart is broken," Kristina said, clutching her own, her form still shimmering blue.

I rolled my eyes, upset that I'd built up Jack's day and then torn it down so quickly. "You don't have a heart."

"Shut up, Baylor."

TIP

18

Turning a piece of your soul into a metaphysical object is exactly as hard as it sounds.

MOM HAD TO CHASE DOWN MINH AND Adam to stop them from running off into the night by themselves. Once she wrangled them, she couldn't persuade the boys to come back inside the house, so she wound up dropping them off at Minh's house since Cam was done with his movie anyway.

Then there was the whole matter of the ghosts who'd shown up to deliver a cryptic warning. Kristina was lying on my bed, spent from the massive amount of energy she'd used expelling them from the house.

"How could you not know what they meant?" I

asked, frantically lighting as many candles as I could find. "How could you not know who they were?"

"I don't know, Baylor," she said, sounding weak. "Clearly it's never happened before."

"Shouldn't you be in the Beyond asking some questions?"

"I will tonight," she said. "But right now, I just want to rest and think."

"But they said I need to be careful! Careful about what?!"

"I'm not sure."

"They said a change is coming, Kristina!" I said, placing a third candle on the windowsill. "My soul is at stake?" I peered out the window, half expecting to see a Bruton or something worse staring back at me. "That sounds *pretty* bad if you ask me."

"Baylor, I can assure you, you're perfectly safe," Colonel Fleetwood said. "Nothing to worry about."

"Did we not just live through the same fiasco, Fleetwood? You're joking right?"

"Clearly they were just trying to scare you."

"Actually, *you're* scaring me," I said, throwing my hands up, "because you're not taking this seriously. How did they enter the house? What happened to the protections?"

"They were actually the boys' relatives," he said

with a shrug. "We could feel it. That kind of connection can't be faked."

"So then my little brother's friends"—ha! Friends. Poor Jack was never going to have friends after those boys told everyone about what they experienced— "conveniently both had relatives with special powers in the Beyond?"

He shook his head. "I didn't feel any negative energy. They were being influenced by someone in the Beyond," he said. "No doubt about that. The main question is, quite simply, why?"

"Yes, Colonel," I said, turning slowly to look at him. "That literally is the main question we've been trying to address here. Such incredible insight on your part!"

"Baylor," Kristina said, sitting up, "stop it."

"No," I said, feeling myself grow livid, "because maybe you don't have all the answers, but *he* should. He's one of our spirit guides, and he shouldn't be standing here, twiddling his thumbs, while you're the one taking care of threatening visitors."

"If he'd taken care of them," she said pointedly, "and I hadn't, that would have made me look really, really bad."

"Do you . . . do you think anything here made you look good?"

"If I hadn't taken action, the Higher Powers in the Beyond would have noticed," she said, standing up, "and they would have held it against me that I didn't fight back when you felt endangered."

"But why was I in danger in the first place? Our protections are in place, and you all are here—even Uncle Charlie."

"Hey!" he said.

"Really? Come on," I said. He glared at me.

"Baylor, do you think there's an invisible brick wall or something between you and the other side?" Kristina asked.

"What? No. But I mean, you guys are here, and I'm wearing this dumb necklace, so that should be enough to stop anything from crossing over."

She threw her head back in laughter. "You can't be serious. Baylor, the other side is just there," she said, exasperated, throwing her arms out around her. "It's everywhere. We can do our best to protect you from the evil, but we can't possibly protect you from everything that feels like stopping by for a visit. If something more powerful from the other side wants to send you a message, then guess what? You're getting the message."

"What?" I said, dazed.

"Baylor, after the Rosalie incident, it was clear

things were changing," she said. "Your powers are growing, and mine are too, and everything we've known for the last couple years is going to start changing. Okay?" She put her head into her hands and seemed to squeeze hard. "I'm sorry. I should have spelled this out earlier, but I didn't know how, and I still don't really know the extent of what that means." She turned my way, her eyes wide and desperate. "But look, Baylor, just this week you're suddenly walking through dreams and communicating with kids who are floating in an ocean hundreds of miles away. It's happening so fast."

Colonel Fleetwood flitted over and ghost-hugged her, which was an odd thing to witness. Ghosts hugged by submerging their bodies into each other, so they essentially morphed into one figure for a few seconds.

"Okay," I said after a few seconds, "enough of that." They didn't move. "Separate!" I said while clapping hard.

Kristina turned to me and glared. "We're hugging, Baylor. What's the issue?"

"You've just gotta, you know, leave room for the Holy Spirit, right?" I scrunched up my face. "Looked a little tight to me."

She sighed and freed herself from the colonel's

grip. "I don't even have the energy to hate you," she said. "I feel so awful for Jack. I really think we may have ruined his childhood. He's going to grow up and be one of those people who works silently behind a desk and then goes home to his studio apartment and heats up frozen gas station burritos for dinner and doesn't interact with humans. We've ruined him."

"That's not gonna happen," I said.

She shook her head, her eyes wide. "I hope not."

There was a weird pause as we considered Jack's future, but then a wave of tiredness hit me and I was elated. Finally—the day was over. I could go to sleep, and wake up in the morning and not feel so bad about things.

"Are you all heading to the Beyond, or are you keeping watch in the night?"

"Well," Kristina said dryly, "apparently it doesn't even matter anymore, so . . ." She shrugged. "Good luck."

I had a feeling she was kidding, but I wasn't 100 percent sure.

"Are . . . are you putting up other protections?"

"Baylor," she said, "you'll be fine for tonight. Just be careful if you go dreamwalking." She paused. "Better yet, just exhibit some self-control and don't go dreamwalking for once. That would solve a lot of issues, actually."

I waved them good night while chuckling to myself. Self-control? Was she forgetting I needed to somehow leave a piece of my soul with Archie and Helena? I was in for a long night.

I thought I'd be tossing and turning and restless in bed all night, but I somehow wound up falling asleep in only a few seconds. I found myself in the middle of an ocean, along with my family and friends, practicing for our upcoming swim meet.

"Just twenty more miles until we reach the shore!" J said between strokes.

"That's nothing," my dad called out. "This is a piece of cake compared to teaching math to some of my students."

Waves thrashed around us, and for some reason I was perfectly content to glide forward through the waves, to pretend I was a dolphin and be one with the ocean. It was peaceful in a way.

"Okay, we're entering Shark City," Bobby called out.

That got my attention.

"What?!" I said, suddenly snapping to attention and noticing the hundreds of fins cutting through the water ahead of us. "Why would we swim through that?"

One of the sharks popped up through the water, its expression deeply pained.

"We're not all vicious, Baylor," it said. "You shouldn't judge a book by its cover."

"Don't make me feel bad," I said, "I'm really stressed out right now, and sharks don't exactly have the best track record, you know."

"So you're going to judge all of us based on the actions of a few?" it said. "That's a horrible thing to do."

"It seems logical to me."

"We don't even like the taste of humans," it said. "You taste like rotten tuna fish cans."

"How would you know that?"

It shrugged casually. "I made some mistakes in my youth," it said, "but what's important"— it leaned forward and stared deeply into my eyes—"is that I've changed."

"I don't have time to talk about this!" I snapped, remembering I was on a mission. "I shouldn't be talking to you at all. You're a shark! I need to go talk to Archie and Helena!" I hunched into a ball, sprang up, and dolphin-leaped out of the water and through the air, somersaulting onto Loved Ones' Lane.

"Dang righteous sharks," I muttered as I sprinted down the black lane, the shooting stars twinkling around me, "wasting all my time."

As I reached the end of the lane, I ran a little faster and plunged off the edge, doing a little flip on my way down into the ocean. I swam in the normal direction, unimpeded by activist sharks, and arrived at the boat, where Archie and Helena lay unmoving, their bodies rocking along with the waves. A chill passed through my body; they looked like corpses.

"Archie?" I called out, pulling myself onto the boat. "Helena?"

They both stirred lightly. "Baylor?" Archie said. "That you?"

"Yes," I said, not sure of what to do. Archie's skin had somehow taken on a sickly pallor, and with the light of the moon illuminating his face, he looked like he'd been stuck in an industrial freezer. The light was doing other weird tricks, too, as it seemed to shimmer around us in different colors and light up both the space just around the boat and the sky, like otherworldly heat lightning.

"What is that?" I asked, mesmerized. It was like the aurora borealis was deciding to show off just for us. The thought crossed my mind that maybe they were auroras, that Archie and Helena had drifted so far north they'd arrived in Iceland. But that couldn't be—they'd have suffered the effects of hypothermia by now.

"What's what?" he asked, his voice low and tired. It seemed a miracle he could say anything at all.

"The lights," I said. "Can't you see them?"

He gave a cursory turn of the head, but didn't move otherwise. "I see only the dark."

"Weird," I said, "anyway, listen, I might have figured out a way to find you, but it's not going to be easy."

"What is it?" he asked, suddenly sounding more alert. "Can I help?"

"I don't think so," I said, genuinely not sure what he could do to rip off a piece of my soul. "This is going to sound weird, but . . . but I need to leave a piece of my soul here."

He furrowed his brows, silent for a few seconds, until he said, "You mean like in Harr—"

"No!" I said, "not like that. I thought the same thing, though."

"Oh, good," he said, sounding relieved. "I thought you were about to kill me or something for a second there."

"What! No!"

"And the worst part," he said with a whisper, "is that I almost felt happy about it."

I didn't know what to say. I couldn't imagine how he felt. He was so thirsty, so hungry, so broken and battered, to the point where the thought of dying sounded ideal. I gulped. I needed to figure out this whole soul situation tonight.

I thought about the happy summers at my grandparents' house and tried to imagine myself there, and apply that same feeling to this setting. This dark, desolate setting, where the only objects in sight were an overturned boat and two kids who were one powerful wave away from drowning.

"How can I make this a happy memory?" I said, feeling genuinely frustrated. "It's impossible."

"You have to think past the water," Archie said. "If you don't, everything will slip away."

"What have you been thinking about?"

Archie hesitated, but a small smile crossed his face. "My parents. The memories seem so far away and so close at the same time." He tried to lick his lips, but his mouth was so dry that it was pointless. "I keep thinking of when I was younger, and I used to go running to my parents' room, and I'd dive into their bed." He stopped, his voice getting rougher. "And they'd snuggle with me forever and make an Archie Sandwich. And then we'd eat breakfast and play outside. They'd run through the sprinklers with me, over and over, and we'd make Slip 'N Slides, and throw water balloons in the pool." He swallowed loudly. "I miss them so much, Baylor."

I had tears in my eyes but didn't know what to do.

"I'm so sorry, Archie," I said, wiping my eyes. I sat down and touched his shoulder. "I passed on your message. They know you're alive. Just keep holding on. We'll figure this out."

He swallowed again, but it took a huge effort, like he was trying to push down a golf ball. "I'm trying, Baylor."

"I know," I said. "And I am too." What on earth was I going to do? Why hadn't I pestered Madame Nadirah for some soul scissors or something to try to cut off a piece of my soul? It sounded painful, but hopefully it'd be as easy as getting a haircut. This whole thought process was absurd; I couldn't cut something that wasn't solid. It'd be like trying to slice smoke.

I spent a few minutes trying out different things in case I felt a piece of my soul break: meditation, praying, squeezing every muscle in my body in an attempt to push it out, rocking back and forth (which I quickly realized was an awful idea as the boat began to move with me—I may as well have just pushed Archie and Helena off the boat myself and called it a day).

But there was nothing to be done. I couldn't just

will myself into leaving a part of my soul here. That's not how it worked.

"I'll figure this out," I said, feeling desperate on their behalf. "I promise. I'll figure it out."

Using all his energy, Archie lifted up his head and smiled. "Thank you for trying, Baylor. See you soon."

I nodded and jumped into the ocean to swim back to Loved Ones' Lane, considering all my options.

I could try again with Madame Nadirah. Maybe she had researched more for me, or perhaps she could reach out to any of her mystic friends, if she had any. I wasn't sure if she did. I didn't think there were any national conferences for the spiritually gifted, but I'd also never researched it.

I could ask Kristina to demand someone on the other side do something about this. It was ridiculous—surely they could help. But I already knew they wouldn't. There were so many other people who were suffering and needed help. They wouldn't give special dispensation for these two just because I'd asked for it.

I could fly down to Florida and see if I could actually be of use to Archie and Helena's families. The fact that I was even seeing Archie and Helena was weird enough on its own; maybe being surrounded by their families would help bolster my powers? The thought of flying on a commercial airplane made me shudder, though.

Perhaps the amulet would help, but being trapped in a flying tube with a couple hundred other people, and their many, many dead relatives would feel like flying in a very large and very packed sardine can.

I ran out of ideas by the time I was back on the lane, and I walked back to home base slowly, hoping another idea would pop into my brain. Nothing happened, of course.

I was planning on returning to my dream and getting some rest—maybe that would help spur ideas—when I passed Aiden's door. The shooting stars were so bright, like the light bulbs had been replaced, that I was tempted for a moment to see what he was dreaming about.

No. No, I couldn't possibly. I'd already done it once and was sure he was suspicious of me, even though he had no real reason to suspect anything.

I was about to head through my door when I stopped again. He had been so mad today, strutting off to who knows where and not returning any of our texts and calls. Maybe it wouldn't be a bad thing to check in? In fact, I considered it a necessary friend duty, just to make sure everything was all right.

Convinced, I doubled back, somersaulted through the door, and immediately realized I'd made a huge mistake.

Elaborate lies *can* save friendships. Sometimes.

I WAS STUCK. LITERALLY. I COULDN'T MOVE.
I was trapped in some kind of bizarre black space,
through which a massive tangle of intricate, white
webbing sliced the air every which way. The threads
were thin and delicate-looking, but they were taut and
strong. I was effectively a bug caught in a spider's
massive web. My wrists and legs were bound in the
threads and ribbons and beads surrounding me.

At first I thought it was part of Aiden's dream, but
then I noticed, just beyond the edge of the ribbons,
I could see Aiden's dream playing out as though it

were on a projection screen. I couldn't access it for some reason.

Panic gripped me. I thought of my interaction earlier with Minh's and Adam's relatives, about things changing and my soul being in danger and my need to be careful. What if this is what they were referring to? What if I'd just made it extremely easy for a demon to come wrap me up in some weird dream thread and save me for that night's dinner?

I started beating my hands and legs against the threads, hoping I could free myself, but they were extremely durable. I wasn't going anywhere. I thought of those soul scissors I'd wanted on the boat—boy, those would have been useful right about now. I made a mental note to ask Madame Nadirah if something like that existed.

I looked around, wondering if there was something else that could help. I felt a vibration on the thread and turned my head to the right. Something was moving over there; an invisible source was causing it. My mind went to the worst place: I imagined demon spiders crawling across the webbing to come eat me. I imagined an army of Brutons flapping their wings, ready to burn me to a crisp with their fiery eyes. I imagined the return of the Sheet Man, some new terror to come haunt me.

I tensed my muscles, trying to pull a Kristina and send

a surge of blue energy through me to slice through the threads, but nothing happened. The vibrations increased, and so did my panic. This was it. I was so dumb. How could I not have listened to those ghosts? I was done for; I hadn't exhibited any of the self-control Kristina advised me to use. Ugh, I *hated* when she was right—especially during the times I found myself trapped in a giant web and about to die. I shut my eyes, and tried one last time to rip my arms from the threads.

"Baylor?"

I unclenched my eyes and saw Tommy Thorne hovering in front of me, lit up in light-blue energy. Tommy was forever a cool fourth grader, with his long, side-swept black hair and a permanent friendly smirk on his face. He'd died in a car crash in fourth grade, but we'd remained friendly on the other side.

"Tommy!" I said. "What are you doing here?"

"I was on the Lane visiting my dad and noticed Aiden's light going berserk," he said with a shrug. "I wanted to see what was going on."

"Thank *God* you're here," I said, unbearably relieved. "Can you help me?"

He laughed. "What? You don't need my help."

I frowned. "What are you talking about? I'm trapped here."

"Baylor"—he said my name as though my brain

were slower than a turtle swimming through molasses—
"just wake up."

"What?"

"You're not trapped here forever," he said. "All you have to do is stop sleeping. It's pretty simple."

"Wait," I said. "Seriously?"

"Seriously," he said, nodding.

"Oh." And I shut my eyes, forced some blood into my head, and pushed myself awake.

I sat up in bed, rubbing my wrists. It felt like they'd been in handcuffs.

Tommy joined me in my room, hovering over Jack and Oli. They were nearer to his size than I was; he was forever four-and-a-half-feet tall.

"That was bizarre," I said. "Why didn't you get trapped?"

"I was ready for it," he said, holding up his hand and flaring some blue energy.

"Weird. It's almost like Aiden put up some kind of protection."

"I'm sure he did. It—"

"Baylor," whispered Oli in a terrified voice, "can you please stop whatever you're doing?"

"Sorry, Oli," I said. "Go back to sleep."

I looked at Tommy and rolled my eyes. *Sorry*, I mouthed. He grinned.

"See ya later."

I'd managed to fall back asleep, carefully avoiding dipping into any more dreams for the rest of the night, but woke up early to distressed texts from J.

> J: Still feeling so bad about Aiden

> J: I know he's ignoring me. He usually takes ~4 seconds to answer

> J: We need to do something.

> BAYLOR: Like what?

> J: Something that'll make him feel good.

> BAYLOR: We could send over some pepperoni sandwiches.

> J: No. Something BIGGER. I have a crazy idea . . .

We wrangled a plan together, looping in Bobby, and somehow she managed to get ahold of Aiden to persuade him to join her downtown.

"He said he was planning on heading in this direction anyway," she said as we waited together in the square. "He bought a dream catcher from Madame Nadirah yesterday, and he wants to get a refund since it broke overnight."

My eyes widened as I put the pieces together. Aiden had gotten a dream catcher yesterday! No wonder I couldn't visit his dreams: I'd been caught in its web. I made a mental note to tell Madame Nadirah she was selling a dangerous product.

"Baylor," Kristina said, her voice dripping with annoyance, "why did Aiden's dream catcher break?"

Aiden would be arriving any second, so I pretended not to hear her. We waved at Bobby, who was waiting behind a corner, dressed in all black, a ski mask on his head and ready to be pulled down into position for when Aiden arrived.

This really was an insane plan, but J had insisted it would work.

"He just needs a confidence boost," she'd said. "This'll be the simplest way to do it. And maybe we can even get him on the news. You know some people, right?"

"They know me," I said. "I don't know them."

"Still," she said lightly, "we could get ahold of them somehow and mention your name . . ."

I mumbled something about baby steps before hanging up. Honestly, the last thing I needed was any more press coverage.

"Oh, he's coming," J said, excited. "I feel so nervous! I hope this goes smoothly."

There was a huge chance this could end disastrously, but I didn't tell her that.

"This is going to end disastrously," Kristina said next to me. "Colonel Fleetwood even placed a bet on it with Charlie. Odds are five-to-one that Aiden breaks a bone."

Aiden sauntered across the street, his head down and his hands in his pockets.

"Hey guys," he said, standing a few feet from where we sat on a bench.

"Hi, Aiden," J said, standing up to hug him. "Having a good morning?"

He shook his head. "I spent fifteen bucks on this piece of crap yesterday," he said, pulling out the splintered remains of his dream catcher. "And I wake up this morning to see it's snapped in half. Look!"

I ignored Kristina's glare and examined the object, half expecting to see a Baylor-shaped hole in the threads. The wooden hoop around which the threads were tied was cracked in two places, directly opposite from each other. The webbing remained intact for the most part, minus the ripped threads near the severed parts of the hoop.

"Is there a chance you accidentally broke it in your sleep?" I asked.

"Doubtful," he said. "I sleep with a bunch of blankets, so my arms don't really have room to reach out and grab things." I imagined Aiden swaddled like a giant baby.

"That's a bummer," I said, doing my best to suppress my smile.

"Yeah, go figure," he said, shoving the dream catcher back into his pocket. "Of course it would happen to me."

We turned to walk in the direction of Madame Nadirah's shop, and J hiked up her purse and subtly double-tapped the back of her head, giving Bobby the signal they'd come up with.

"I'm sure it won't be a problem to get a new one," J said. Behind her, Bobby pulled down his black ski mask and was quietly jogging up behind us.

"Yeah, I'll make sure Madame Nadirah helps you," I said. "We go way back."

"Yeah, way back to like three weeks ago, Baylor," J said. "You've had a longer relationship with your toothbrush."

"Don't dis my toothbrush like that," I said, just as Bobby approached us.

Like they'd rehearsed, he gave J a good shove, grabbed her purse, and took off sprinting.

Well, that's what he was supposed to do, at least.

In the excitement of the moment, he'd pushed J too hard and she shrieked, flying forward and hitting the ground on top of her bag. Aiden and I stood there, stunned, as Bobby ran past us, jumping rapidly from side to side around her fallen form, and tried to figure out how to steal the bag from underneath J, especially since it was still looped around her shoulder.

Aiden yelled, "What are you doing!" as Bobby started tugging at the bag to pull it loose. It was stuck around J and too awkward to remove without manhandling her. He looked at me, then Aiden, confusion and panic shining from his eyes through his ski mask. J, thankfully, realized the problem and shifted her body around so the purse would be easy to grab, and with one last valiant tug, Bobby took hold of the purse, jumped gleefully into the air, and skipped away.

"Come back here!" Aiden yelled after him.

"Chase him, Aiden!" I yelled. "I'll stay with J and make sure she's okay."

"But you're faster than me."

"I . . . I . . . I hurt my foot last night and can't run?" I stammered, trying to think of anything that made sense. "I was playing Twister with Jack and his friends and got too confident and fell while reaching for a red circle." He was staring at me in confusion while J stared at me like she would start beating me senseless, if only she still had her bag.

"Oh wow," Kristina said. Her hands were plastered over her eyes, but she was watching through small gaps between her fingers. "Oh, this is just awful."

"Go, Aiden!" I said, turning to look at Bobby, who was about fifty yards away. He had slowed to a jog and kept looking at us over his shoulder, unsure of what to do. "He's getting away!"

"I can't!" Aiden said, looking at the masked man running further and further down the road.

J took hold of his hand, gripped tightly, and said, "Yes, you can, Aiden. I believe in you."

Aiden's mouth dropped open slightly and he took a sharp breath. Suddenly, he set his shoulders back, clenched his jaw, and nodded, his face fierce and determined. He got up and ran toward Bobby, who sprang back into action when he saw Aiden heading his way.

"Not too fast, Bobby!" I said, under my breath.

"But not so slow it's easy for Aiden to catch him," J said breathlessly.

"Medium pace, Bobby, medium pace," I said, changing my tune. "How's that elbow?"

"I think I'll have a nice bruise, but it's fine," she said. "That moron pushed me way too hard."

"I think he got caught up in the heat of the moment," I said.

"Obviously," she said, rubbing her elbow. "And it nearly ruined the plan."

Nearly being the pivotal word. Aiden found his inner gazelle and, faster than I would have ever thought possible, was within spitting distance of Bobby. Bobby realized it, too, and shrieked in surprise. He threw the purse back at Aiden in an effort to stave him off, and hit him right in the face.

"Gah!" Aiden screamed, and even one downtown square and a few blocks away, we could hear a distinct *crunch* as the bag hit his nose.

"*Ooh!*" J and I gasped in unison as we watched Aiden catch the bag and bend over, his hands clutching his nose.

There was a silent moment in which Bobby ran off toward the cemetery down the road, Aiden continued to suffer alone, and J and I grimaced in Aiden's direction.

Then J stood up and shouted, deep from her diaphragm, "You did it, Aiden! Thank you, thank you!"

"Go, Aiden!" I shouted. "You showed him!"

Aiden stood up straight, his hands still covering his nose, and looked our way. We didn't have a clear view of his face, but it was obvious he was thrilled by our reactions. He slowly sauntered our way, and J met him in the middle of the square.

"My hero!" she crooned, pulling him into a hug.

He wore a dumb smile on his bright red face, and he raised his eyebrows excitedly in my direction, his entire neck flexing and rolling in excitement. Charlie and the colonel were crowding around them as Charlie shouted, "Rigged! The entire thing was rigged!"

"You knew that going in," the colonel said, bemused, as Charlie handed over some weird-looking ghost money. I made a mental note to ask Kristina about that later.

"Got lucky, ya did," he said bitterly as the colonel pocketed his ghost money. "That porker shoulda fell."

"Charlie!" Kristina said, her voice appearing to lash into Charlie, who recoiled as though his entire body had touched a hot pan. "Don't be rude."

I cocked my head at her, confused. "Only I get to make fun of Aiden," she said with a light shrug. "And you, for that matter."

"Should we call the police or something?" Aiden asked, his voice nasally from how tightly his hand covered his face.

"No!" J said quickly. "It's fine."

"But what if he does it to someone else?"

"I have a feeling you scared him off," she said.

He frowned. "Are you joking?"

"No!" she said. "Seriously, I think it's some punk neighborhood kid, and I bet he thought you wouldn't chase after him. But you did! I'm sure he's hiding behind some tombstone in the cemetery, praying you won't come looking for him."

He shrugged. "Maybe."

J smiled. "Definitely." Then she frowned as she got a good look at his nose. "I think you need to go to the hospital, though."

We headed to Madame Nadirah's shop first, though, so Aiden could get his refund, but she was reluctant to give him one.

"It worked!" she said. "It protected you. It sacrificed itself to keep a threat from invading your dreams."

"I thought it was a permanent thing, not a one-time use," he said.

"It depends on the threat," she said, glancing at me for a split second. We made eye contact and I blushed, heading over to look at the candles. "Whatever was trying to invade last night was very powerful."

He frowned. "Well, if you're not giving me my money back, can I least get a replacement one?"

She eyed me suspiciously again, but turned back to him and appraised his broken nose with a pitying smile.

"Sure thing, my dear. I just hope those big powerful threats mind their own business from now on."

J and Aiden headed to the hospital, and I had to rush to the house to have lunch with Uncle Glenn, Gillie, and Oli before they headed home. The entire bike ride back, Kristina gave me an earful about dream-walking and my stupid decisions. I didn't say a word, letting her talk until she finally ran out of things to say.

"Your ears still workin' all right after all tha'?" Charlie asked me.

"Shut your mouth, One-Buck Chuck," she spit.

"Oy!" he said, wounded. "I was jus' jokin'!"

This had been one of the more disastrous holidays, and I was looking forward to them leaving so we could put the whole incident behind us.

Back at home, Uncle Glenn squeezed my shoulders and gave me a tight hug as he headed out the door with a small mountain of bags. "See you soon, little buddy."

Gillie wasn't exactly warm as she said good-bye. To my surprise, she went in for a hug too, but it was just so she could whisper, "Thanks again for ruining my life, Baylor" quietly into my ear.

I let go of her and patted her on the back. "Best

of luck to you, Gillie. I'm sure the rest of your time in high school is going to be just fantastic for the rest of us."

Oli squeezed me into a bear hug. "I'll miss you, Baylor," he said. "But I won't miss hearing you talk to ghosts in the middle of the night."

Jack's face fell into horror. "What?"

I tried to laugh it off. "Ha-ha nothing, Oli's just kidding. Bye, Oli, see you later," I said, shoving the kid out the door.

"There was a ghost in your room last night?" he asked.

"Jack, there's always a ghost in my room," I said. "Kristina? Remember?"

His face was still sunken, but he didn't say anything else.

"Well," Kristina said, eyeing his expression, "I guess I'll have to reevaluate my feelings on Jack."

I kept my mouth shut since I was already on thin ice with him, but she read my eyes.

"I know he's freaked out by ghosts," she said with an annoyed tone, "but come on! I'm his sister!"

That afternoon I hung out in the family room and played with Ella, who was really into grabbing things over and over again and then trying to eat them. My shirt, my phone, the remote control, the empty bag of chips by my side, her various toys—anything and everything was up for grabs.

She'd fallen asleep after a couple hours, and I turned on the TV. Except, as I flipped through the channels, I realized I was just trying to get to a news station for any updates on Archie and Helena.

I found a news channel and waited through a whole cycle of news before it started to repeat, with no mention of the lost kids. Demon dung. I didn't know what I was hoping for. It seemed like we needed a miracle at this point.

I looked at Ella, sleeping quietly, and suddenly felt exhausted myself. It'd been an exciting, tumultuous morning, and my brain was demanding some rest. I sat back and closed my eyes.

Seconds later, I was floating through the air, hovering over Loved Ones' Lane.

Well, that's weird, I thought. *Am I dreaming about the lane or am I already there?*

It began to feel too complicated to think about what was happening, so I just went with the flow, sailing down the lane, past the edge overlooking the vast ocean, which was sparkling brightly under the sun. Except it was too strangely bright, and the odd shimmering colors from last night were more vibrant than ever.

What's going on? What's with all the weird light?

Suddenly it became pitch-black, and the ocean and the blue sky and the sun vanished.

Where had the light gone?

I looked around me and noticed the rectangle shape again in the distance, so I ventured toward it. The thin band of light coming around the sides seemed to grow brighter as I approached it, and it dawned on me the light must have gone to the other side of the door. All I had to do was open it to make this side bright again. Easy peasy.

I leisurely floated over, reached out to the door handle, and, just as I about to turn the knob, was blasted backward in a blazing pulse of light.

I woke with a gasp and looked around the family room.

Ella was still sleeping, a glob of drool yo-yoing from her mouth.

Kristina was there, looking at me in confusion.

And Archie was there, standing in front of us, smiling sadly.

He'd crossed over to the other side.

TIP

20

Flying private isn't that glamorous.

"NO," I SAID, STANDING UP QUICKLY. "NO!" Tears brimmed at my eyes. "If you're here now, that means . . ."

"There's nothing more to be done, Baylor," he said. "It's too late for me."

Ella woke up and blinked rapidly, her eyes focusing on the new boy in the room.

"Bay-Bay?" she said, uncertain.

"Ella, that's Archie," I said, my voice breaking.

"Archie!" she squeaked.

Somehow I managed to laugh; Ella's cuteness was

the only saving grace in the face of this tragic discovery.

He smiled at her. "She reminds me of my little sister," he said. I thought of when I heard him singing "Amazing Grace," how he mentioned his little sister playing peekaboo to the lyrics. A pang of sadness flitted in my stomach.

"Are you okay, Archie?" Kristina asked, standing up to greet her fellow ghost. "Sometimes it can be shock for newcomers."

"I feel okay," he said. "I'm mostly happy I'm not hungry anymore."

"This is horrible," I said. "First you, and Helena will likely be here soon."

"No," he said, his voice suddenly fierce. "It may have been too late for me, but it's not too late for her. You can still save her."

"How?" I said, perking up. "Can you lead the way?"

"I wouldn't need to," he said. "You could find her even without me."

Kristina's eyebrows shot up. "You don't mean . . . it worked?"

Archie nodded. "You've left a piece of your soul there, Baylor."

I frowned. "Are you messing with me?"

"Of course not," he said. "You must have teared up while I was talking about my parents, leaving a piece of your soul on the boat."

"I don't know," I muttered. "It was only one, maybe two tears."

"And that's how you're here now, then?" Kristina said. "Because of the soul connection with Baylor the Crybaby?"

"Archie told a really sad, touching story," I said, flustered.

Archie nodded. "I wouldn't normally be able to connect with him?"

She shook her head. "Baylor's power is proximity based, more out of necessity than anything else. Otherwise, just think of how many people and spirits would be trying to reach him from all over the world."

"Well, only one person matters right now," he said. "Baylor, you have to find Helena. She doesn't have much time."

I hopped off the couch. "I know what to do."

I called Mr. Papadopoulos and explained the situation. He did not sound good.

"Archie's dead?" he said through muffled heaves. "No, no," he cried. "How can this be?"

"Listen, Mr. Papadopoulos, I'm sorry, but you need to pull yourself together," I said sternly. "Who knows how long Helena has? I need to get on a plane right now so I can track her down."

"I'm sorry," he said, coughing and trying to sound calm. "You're absolutely right. I'll call the search team now to arrange the details." He explained that a couple of his friends owned their own small planes and had been aiding in the search. That'd likely be the fastest way to get where we needed to go.

"Call me as soon as you know something."

After we hung up, I had to find my parents and tell them I was making an impromptu trip south.

My mom scoffed. "Like heck you are," she said. "You're not going anywhere."

"Mom, a girl's life is at stake!" I said. "Archie's already dead, and she'll be dead soon if I don't help find her."

She narrowed her eyes. "There's got to be another way."

"There isn't," I said. "If there was, I would have already helped find them."

"But . . . but Baylor, you're just a kid," she said, her eyes bulging. "You shouldn't have to worry about stuff like this."

I blinked, unsure of what to say. "I'm sorry?"

She sighed. "That's not what I meant. You don't need to be sorry," she said. "It's not your fault." She looked at Dad, who was paralyzed by the news, and said, "If anything, it's our fault."

He nodded lightly. "So what now, Baylor?"

"I'm waiting for a call," I said. "One of the volunteers is going to fly us down. Apparently it's a small plane and the turbulence gets pretty bad, but don't worry, I have it on good authority the plane won't crash."

My mom patted my dad on the arm and smiled. "Sounds like a good time for some father-son bonding," she said. "Enjoy the flight."

My dad and I each packed an overnight bag—this wasn't going to be a long trip. All we really needed was a toothbrush and a change of underwear, but we each packed a spare shirt out of decency.

Our pilot was a man named Scott Alvarez who'd been flying planes since he was sixteen years old. He'd known Mr. Papadopoulos since their freshman year of college, and he'd taken the last week off of work to fly around all day along with the coast guard and some other volunteer pilots.

And it just so happened his wife, Jenni, who'd joined him on the flight up, was a huge Bayliever.

As we were prepping for takeoff from the local airport—which was so small that only little planes were landing and taking off, and deer occasionally ran across the runway—Jenni asked me nonstop questions about what is was like to be Boy Wonder Baylor Bosco, the thirteen-year-old medium whose gift has been dominating headlines.

"It's really not that exciting," I said as Scott performed his preflight safety inspection with Colonel Fleetwood hovering over his shoulder, carefully watching his every move. "I mostly just tell people random things their dead relatives say."

"But it's amazing, Baylor," Jenni said, brushing back her blond bangs for the twentieth time in less than five minutes. "I honestly think you must be one of the most gifted people living on the planet right now. I mean, you have a lifeline to Heaven! You could change the world with this gift."

"I'm not trying to change the world," I said, shrugging. "I'm just trying to help people live their lives better."

"Aw!" she said, with a sharp exhale of breath, covering her heart. "And that humble attitude is why you're going to make such a difference."

"This is disgusting to watch," Kristina said, appearing next to me. "Charlie just tried to bet Colonel Fleetwood that she was going to ask you for your autograph, but he didn't understand the concept of an autograph, so the whole thing fizzled out." She pursed her lips. "I still think she's going to, though."

"So what's it like?" Jenni said in a hushed tone, suddenly leaning in, like she was about to partake in some big secret. "What do ghosts look like?"

"They really don't look any different than living people," I said. "That's why it can be tricky sometimes. I've had to learn to tune them out so I don't get confused."

"Are they wearing the same clothes they had on when they died?" she asked.

"No, they can change their clothes," I said. Kristina, for example, often wore shirts with different animals on them. When I'd asked her why, she said something about not being able to have her own pets, so the shirts made up for it. The conversation had ended abruptly, though, because when I told her that logic didn't make any sense, she told me to can it.

"They change their clothes? So I'll finally be able to wear Chanel?" Her eyebrows flew up. "I'll just have to be dead?" She threw her head back in laughter. "Well, that's comforting."

"All set," Scott said. "You gents ready to go?"

Dad was eyeing the sky, checking for any storm clouds. "We're sure this is an all right time to fly? Not better to wait until morning when there's daylight?"

"Drew, there is a girl's life at stake," Scott said, still examining his clipboard and marking things off at random. "We can't afford to wait."

"The name's Doug, actually. And I understand that, but it wouldn't make sense to put four more lives at stake if it's not safe."

"I've been flying planes for thirty years, Dan," said Scott, still going to town on his clipboard. "It's safe out here. Believe me."

"Again, it's *Doug*," my dad said through gritted teeth.

"Righty-oh," said Scott, signing the paper on the clipboard with a big flourish. "I'll drop off the paperwork and we'll be all set to go. Jenni, help the guys load in."

The plane was tiny—my mom's minivan may have had it beat—and she directed us to the tight backseat.

"Scott likes me to act as his copilot," she said, brushing her bangs back again. "We make a great team."

"It's . . . cozy," my dad said.

"Right?" she said. "So much better than flying commercial."

"Sure," he said. "Who enjoys having a bathroom handy when they're stuck in a tight space for a few hours?"

"Oh, we do have a bathroom," she said. Dad and I looked at each other in confusion; unless you got to it by crawling out the window and opening a secret hatch on the outside of the plane, there was no way this thing had a bathroom.

She reached under the seat and pulled out a plastic tub, just like the one we keep in the car for long road trips with Ella.

"I don't think we'll have any room to use it, though," she said, sounding sorry.

"That's really okay," Dad said. "We'll manage."

Scott arrived and started hitting all sorts of buttons. I'd only flown a few times, mostly to Florida, but each time had been more unpleasant than the one before.

On my most recent flight, while returning home from a trip to Florida, there was a family in front of me who apparently very much enjoyed yodeling, and they had gone to Disney World to yodel at the Matterhorn ride since it was less expensive than flying to the real mountain in Switzerland. However, someone didn't do their research properly, because the Matterhorn ride is only at the Disney park in California, not the one in Florida. It was quite the disappointment.

I learned all of this, of course, from their relatives

who 1) talked nonstop and 2) enjoyed yodeling even in the afterlife. ("The acoustics on this side are unreal!") They spent the entire flight performing sad yodels, in solidarity with their relatives, until I couldn't take it anymore. I very quietly and subtly tapped the passenger in front of me on her shoulder and, in one exasperated breath, said, "My name is Baylor Bosco and I can communicate with people who have crossed over, and I'm really sorry but you seem to have lost a lot of people in your life who just love to yodel. They're here now, yodeling nonstop, because they feel bad your husband messed up the trip and took you to the park without the Matterhorn, so please just know they're with you in spirit." I sat back and turned to Kristina, who sealed off the connection with sheer glee. The yodeling stopped, but then the questions from the relatives started, and there was no way to zap them into another dimension—not yet, at least.

Anyway, the point is that flying commercial was best avoided whenever possible, at least until I could exhibit more control over my power. I rubbed the amulet around my neck and wondered whether it had pushed me to another level. For the last week, tuning ghosts out had been far too simple. Minus the whole dreamwalking thing, it felt like I'd been living a relatively normal life. It was sort of nice.

Scott got the plane out onto the runway, and before I knew it we had taken off and were soaring into the dark sky. Luckily tonight there was a full moon, meaning there'd be added protections from any lurking evildoers.

We were wearing headsets to hear one another over the roar of the engine, and Scott said, "Enjoy the flight, everyone. Touchdown in Florida in three hours."

"So, Baylor," Jenni said, "is there anyone trying to communicate with you now?"

I tuned the ghosts in and jumped up in surprise, since some had appeared outside the dashboard window, staring at us through the glass.

"Tell Jenni her hair is *fab*," said an aunt who'd squeezed herself in the empty space between the front and back seats.

I repeated the message, and Kristina sealed off the connection. Jenni, meanwhile, erupted in panic.

"Oh my god, oh my god, oh my god oh my god," she said, gripping her face, her nails digging into her cheeks. "It's happening, Scott, it's happening."

I looked out the windows and counted about twenty relatives. I sighed to myself. Might as well talk to all of them—I had nothing else to do for a few hours.

One by one, each ghost filled the empty space in the plane so I could deliver a message to either Scott or Jenni—and one for Dad, actually, from an old teacher of his from high school who was proud he'd made the leap to teaching.

"I can't believe this is happening," said Jenni, who'd been crying steadily for nearly an hour. "Who knew all these people would have messages for us?"

"I actually had that same sort of realization recently too," I said. "For the other side, the term *loved ones* is used pretty loosely. Your mailman could be a loved one if you talked to him enough, I think."

"Amazing," said Jenni. "Truly amazing. I can't wait to write about this on BaylieversUnited.com."

My cheeks burned deeply while Kristina cackled next to me.

"She can't be serious! Oh, this is too good," she said.

"You go on that website?" I asked.

"All the time," she said. "I love reading about the different messages you deliver. And I loved that they happen just about anywhere. You never know when Baylor Bosco might pop up to change your life." She laughed and threw her hands up quickly. "Case in point! I had no idea this would happen today. Oh, I just feel so great. I feel so light and happy."

I was glad, if embarrassed, that she felt that way, mainly because my dad—who would never verbally admit it—was totally freaked out whenever he got a message from the Beyond. He usually curled up into a ball and retreated inside himself for a while, like a human armadillo, until the feeling of panic passed.

I was amused by Jenni's reaction, but quite suddenly I felt a pull in the deep pit of my stomach. I knew there was nothing wrong with the plane, but there was still something wrong.

"Do you feel that?" I asked Kristina.

She frowned. "Feel what?"

However, Jenni asked the same question at the exact same time.

"Sorry, Jenni, not you, I was talking to my sister."

Jenni tensed up, turning around slowly with her mouth open.

"Wait," she said, "is that Kristina?"

"Um, yeah," I said.

"Kristina is your sister?"

I nodded.

"Oh." She slapped her hands to her face. "My. God." She looked from me to my dad and back to me. "You poor guys. I am so sorry for your loss. But how *amazing* it is you can still communicate with her."

"Oh, she *loves* that I'm dead," Kristina said, rolling her eyes. "Can't you just feel it oozing out of her? She's probably going to tell all her little friends on your freaky fan site about me."

"Jenni, it's not a big deal or anything," I said slowly, "but could you maybe not mention that online or anywhere? Just to keep some privacy for me?"

Jenni nodded very seriously. "I totally understand, Baylor," she said. "Your secret is safe with me." She winked dramatically, like we were best friends, and giggled quietly.

"Oh, she's going to tell everyone now," Kristina said. "She might have forgotten if you hadn't said anything, but now . . ."

"Whatever," I said, shutting off my headset so no one could hear me but Kristina. "I'll deal with it later. The feeling is still tearing at the pit of my stomach."

"What is it exactly?"

"I can't describe it," I said. "It just feels . . . off. Like, I feel like we're doing something wrong, like we've gone off course."

"Then we've gone off course," she said simply. "How do we get back on course?"

"How am I supposed to know?"

"Your soul is sort of the compass here, Baylor," she said.

Archie materialized out of nowhere. "Whoa!" he said. "I wasn't expecting to land in a plane."

"What are you doing here?"

"I could sense something weird and wanted to make sure everything was okay."

"It's not," Kristina said. "Baylor thinks we're headed off course."

"Well, then get back on course."

"Thanks, guys," I said, " really helpful. Hold on." I flipped the switch on my headset. "Hey, Scott, where are we exactly?"

"We're flying over North Carolina," he said. "Shame you can't see anything through the dark. The Smoky Mountains are really something."

I closed my eyes and focused on my connection to the boat. It's a funny thing when I close my eyes. At first I can't see anything; it's just a black void. But then the black fades away and I can see the current scene in its pure state, which means everything looks a bit trippy. I could see my dad's sickly green aura and Jenni's shimmering gold one. The pulsing blue energy around the plane, a protection from the Beyond. And a wispy line of energy out the cockpit window that was veering to the left as we went continued flying straight ahead.

"We need to head east," I said, opening my eyes. "We need to land and head east."

Scott laughed. "No, son, we're heading to Florida,"
he said. "That's where we'll meet up with the rescue
ops."

"You don't understand," I said. "Helena is off the
North Carolina shore; it wouldn't make sense to go
to Florida."

"That's impossible," he said. "The coast guard
looked at the weather patterns and the currents, and
they determined the boat would be headed south."

"Maybe that's why no one has found anything, then,"
I said. "They've been looking in the wrong place."

"Son," Scott said, "believe me, these people know
what they're talking about."

"Scott, I don't want to sound rude right now,
maybe because you're in control of my life at this
exact moment, but Archie is here with us now and
he's telling us we're going the wrong way," I said, feeling only slightly guilty about the lie. If that wouldn't
convince him to land, I wasn't sure what would. "So
you can either believe the coast guard that's been
wrong for the past week, or you can believe the ghost
whose body is still with the girl we're trying to find."

The roar of the engines was the only noise for a
few seconds, until Jenni started hitting Scott's arm.
"*Why aren't you turning yet?*" she said, landing a punch
with every word.

"All right, all right," he said. "It doesn't happen just like that. I can go into a holding pattern, but I need to radio for permission to change the route and request clearance to land at an airport in the area."

"What are you waiting for!" Jenni said, her voice a shriek. "Do it already!"

And so the process to land in North Carolina began. I had no idea so much went into flight planning; the radio back-and-forth, the charting on maps, the careful routing. It was a tedious affair, but ultimately we began our descent.

"Baylor," Scott asked. "What do we need to do once we land? I want to have an idea in my head of what's feasible for tonight. There's a chance we may have to wait until morning since we've diverted so last minute."

"No," Archie growled. "It must be tonight. She's in bad shape."

"It has to be tonight," I said with a nervous gulp. "It'll be too late by morning."

Scott and Jenni exchanged nervous looks, while Dad put his hand on my shoulder and squeezed gently.

"I can radio in requests now," Scott said. "Name it. We'll see what we can get."

"This is crazy," I said, "but we'll need a helicopter."

"The coast guard could have one ready to go in

just a few minutes' notice," he said, a hint of doubt underpinning his voice. "But it'll be up to them."

There was a part of me that knew I could use my gift to strongly influence others. People in positions of power were much more likely to respond to someone who could pass on messages from their dead parents than they were to listen to someone with nothing of value to offer. I didn't love to use my power for that reason, but at this point I was willing to deliver a thousand messages to anyone in the coast guard who would listen to me, so long as they could lend us a helicopter to find Helena.

"If you can get me to the coast guard," I said awkwardly, "I bet I'd be able to convince someone."

Jenni turned to face me, a glint of exhilaration in her eyes. She knew what I was trying to say, and she was loving every second of it. I expected to see a full write-up of the night's events on BaylieversUnited.com in due time.

The next half hour passed by in a blur of confused radio messages. It was clear Scott rarely deviated from his set flight paths, so he was stumbling over all sorts of procedural questions. Jenni did her best to help him, but I had the feeling that, aside from patting him on the back and telling him he was doing a good job, she was pretty useless as a copilot.

Finally we began the descent into Wilmington, a small city on the coast of North Carolina.

"The coast guard will have a car waiting for us there," Scott said. "The base is about ten minutes from the airport."

"That sounds like good news," I said.

He sighed. "We'll see. We've got some connections that got us this far; we'll see how much further they get us."

When we finally landed, a burly coast guard member greeted us on the runway.

"You all go on ahead," Scott said, "we gotta wrap up the plane."

"We're not going?" Jenni screeched.

"This is their thing," Scott said. "Our task is done."

"But I want to watch!"

"That plane ride with all the ghosts and messages wasn't enough for you? You kidding me?"

Jenni pouted, but I didn't say anything. We couldn't waste our time just because of her. Dad and I piled into their SUV, and we were gone in a flash.

21

A ghost's gotta do what a ghost's gotta do.

WHEN WE ARRIVED AT THE COAST GUARD station, I was shocked to find Helios and Dina Papadopoulos waiting for us there.

"Baylor!" Helios said, rising from his chair with surprising ease. He was much older than I was expecting, a cloud of thick, white hair covering his head. Dina's eyes were red and puffy, and she looked like she hadn't slept in week. She probably hadn't. "You made it." He ran over and pulled me into a massive hug. "I don't know how I can ever thank you for this."

"You don't need to," I said. "Let's just find Helena."

Dad introduced himself to Helios, who pulled him into a big hug as well.

"Oh," Dad said. "That's . . . thanks for that."

"You have raised a good son," Helios said. "It's an honor."

Dad smiled. "He takes after his mother."

"How are the Percevals?" I asked, somewhat reluctantly.

His expression sunk. "They are in denial."

"They don't believe it."

He nodded.

"Fair enough," I said. "That's not exactly news anyone wants to get."

"I would have reacted the same way if I were in their shoes," he said quietly. "In these shoes, however, I can still cling to hope."

Dina came up and hugged me as well. "We'll find her, Baylor," she said. "I know we will."

"What are we waiting for?" I asked.

"It should only be a few more minutes now," Helios said. "The Florida coast guard commander is talking to the one here, telling him everything he knows." He looked back at them, almost suspiciously, and turned to me, leaning in. "There is some doubt in the air about the truthfulness of your claims. There seems to be a feeling they shouldn't waste resources chasing leads submitted by children instead of focusing on the solid weather data they've collected."

No surprise there. "I'll talk to whomever needs convincing," I said. "It won't take long."

Helios smiled. "Your confidence," he said. "I like it."

"I'm getting nervous," Kristina said. "They need to hurry up."

"What? That's not good." When Kristina gets nervous, *I* get nervous.

Helios and Dina looked at me strangely.

"Oh, listen, I'm just going to warn you all right now," I said, turning to the people in my immediate vicinity—Dad, Helios, and Dina, and a few coast guard members—"my sister Kristina is here helping us, and I'll be talking to her all night. If it bothers anyone, feel free to walk away." I turned back to Kristina. "Anyway, what's wrong?"

"I can't explain it," she said. "It's almost like a timer was set from the moment Archie crossed over, and I'm just waiting for it to *buzz*, for everything to be too late."

I nodded. "Right. In that case, let's get a move on."

I walked toward the offices in the back of the room—it was a rather cavernous, gray space, with random highlights of the classic coast guard orange here and there.

I knocked on the open door and peeked my head in.

A man in a dark blue jumpsuit was talking on the phone, deep in conversation. The tag on his jumpsuit read BRICKSON.

"Excuse me?" I said politely. "Are we nearly ready to go?"

He looked like he'd never been asked that question before.

"We'll be ready when I say we're ready."

"Can I help with something?" I said, flipping the switch to tune in, and suddenly I felt really bad— Brickson had a lot of immediate family waiting to pass messages. His mom, dad, both sets of grandparents, a sister, several cousins, two aunts, and an uncle.

"Did a tragedy occur in your family?" I said, not thinking about what I was saying, not really speaking to just him anymore. "There are so many young family members here."

"A car accident took five of us out at once," the dad said, nodding. "Talk about a bad day."

"Wow," I said, turning back to Brickson. "Sorry about that."

Now he looked at me as though I'd just swallowed a live rat for fun.

"I . . . I presume you're Baylor Bosco."

"Yep," I said, "and this can go one of a few ways. You'll get to take your pick."

"Stop," he said. "I'm staking my entire career on the line here, son. But I'm willing to do that, and I'll believe you—if you can tell me one thing."

"I'll try," I said.

"What number am I thinking of?"

"What? I can't read minds, that's not—"

But his parents cut me off. "Well, his favorite number is twenty-seven, so that's a good guess," his dad said.

"No, his favorite number is eleven," his mom said. "What are you talking about?"

"His jersey number in college was twenty-seven. He's always loved it."

"But he was born on the eleventh. That's his favorite number, I guarantee it."

"Okay," I said, "I may not be able to read minds, but your parents are helping me out. They can't agree on your favorite number, but they keep going back and forth between eleven and twenty-seven. Is it one of those?"

He dropped his phone. "I was thinking 1,127."

"Not exactly making it easy on me, Brickson."

He picked up the phone. "I have all I need here, Florida. Will report back soon." He hung up, stacked the papers in front of him, and said, "Let's go find Helena."

After a brief safety talk, we loaded into the helicopters. We had to pare down, though, and save spots for the two bodies—one alive, one not—we were hoping to find, leaving room for just me, Dad, Brickson, the pilot, and a rescuer. Helios put up a fight, demanding to go, but Brickson put a stop to it.

"We need to limit the emotional level here," Brickson said. "Believe me, sir—we will do everything we can to find your daughter and bring her back to safety."

Helios was crying, not accepting Brickson's answer, but Dina wrapped her arms around him and pulled him back.

"Onward," Brickson said to the rest of us, stone-faced.

"Are we goin' on that thing, too?" Charlie asked, hesitant. "It seems a bit unstable, don' it? And we'll be over the ocean?"

"No one's forcing you to do anything, Charlie," Kristina said, doing her best to sound polite.

"We have a duty to Baylor," Colonel Fleetwood said, "but you can head back to the Beyond whenever you'd like."

Charlie looked from the colonel to Kristina to me and shook his head.

"Nah," he said. "I've come this far, haven' I? Can' stop now. Ten-Buck Chuck's always up for an adventure, after all!"

I'd never flown on a helicopter before, and I'd be perfectly content never flying on one again. Unlike the usually smooth flight of a plane, every move in a helicopter is obvious and bone-rattling. You could feel every jerk, every turn, every bump caused by something unknown in the air.

Brickson was manning the spotlight, zigzagging the light all over the water below. "Baylor," he said into his headphones—we had to wear them again to hear over the deafening roar of the helicopter blades—"I never say this, and I will never admit to saying this on record should something go wrong tonight, but you're in charge here. Tell us what we need to do."

I looked at Kristina. "Got any tips here?"

She shook her head. "Just follow your soul."

"Great," I said under my breath. More loudly, I said, "Just keep heading east for now."

As we ventured out over the open water, there was a certain charge in the air. I didn't know whether it had something to do with the soul connection, or maybe it was just the familiarity of it from my dreams, or maybe it was just the weather. Regardless, I knew we were on the right path.

"This still doesn't add up to me," Brickson said a few minutes later, lighting up the water below. "It's nearly impossible their boat would have drifted north, let alone this far north."

I wasn't going to argue with coast guard–approved math and data analysis. These guys could outsmart me any day.

"The other side works in mysterious ways, I guess," I said with a shrug.

"Oy," Charlie said quietly, staring intensely at Brickson. "Wait a second . . ."

That's when the helicopter began to shake in a sudden violent way.

"What the—?" my dad yelled into the headset. "What is that?"

"Systems check is clear," the pilot said. "Weather is stable."

Brickson seemed unfazed. "What were you saying about mysteries, Baylor?" he asked with a dark chuckle.

The helicopter jerked to the right in a way that definitely felt unnatural.

"It's them!" Charlie yelped.

"What is that?" I asked, looking from him to Kristina. She, however, was looking out the windows, her eyes tense and fierce.

"I'm such a fool," she said, the tone of her voice a confusing mingling of devastation and determination. "I can't believe I didn't piece this together."

"Kristina, what is it?"

She looked visibly panicked—though not as panicked as Charlie—standing up from the seat next to me, random bursts of blue energy popping from her form.

"It's the Lost Souls, Baylor," she said. "It's been them this whole time."

"What do you mean?"

"They're the reason the wreckage got pulled north," she said.

"The Lost Souls did it?"

"Archie and Helena crossed their path, and they latched onto their boat, pulled it north, and have been waiting to collect their souls," she said. "Except you . . . you interfered somehow. But how?"

"I'm not sure!"

"But then . . . . but why?" she stammered, frantic, as if our lives depended on the what she was thinking. "Has it been a trick this whole time?" She squinted her eyes, trying to piece the puzzle together. "It doesn't make sense. The last week, I've been wondering how you could communicate with Archie and Helena, when there are millions of people suffering around the world. Why could you suddenly talk to them for no apparent reason? Did the Lost Souls form that connection?" She looked like she might pass out, if she could pass out. "Or was it something else?"

I was starting to panic. I had never seen her look so nervous.

"Can you feel them?" she asked, her voice suddenly sharp. "What are we going to do?"

"What do you mean?"

"The Lost Souls, Baylor," she said, "they're coming for us. They'd only wanted Archie and Helena's souls, and now they've got the added bonus of feasting on ours too."

"Arm the defenses," the colonel called out, a blazing white light shining from his sword. He jumped out of the helicopter and landed on the windshield, ready to slay anything that came too close.

I couldn't feel the Lost Souls like they could, but I could feel something else. The memory of Archie talking about his parents was becoming clearer, more vivid, more alive, like a newborn gasping for breath. "We're near Helena, too."

"Of course we are," she said. "It's a trap. They'd stay near to her so they could swoop her up. But why didn't they swoop up Archie?"

"The piece of my soul?" I suggested. "Maybe it's protecting him?"

"It's a possibility," she said.

The helicopter jerked to the left, then the right. Charlie had been standing near the entrance, spreading his blue energy around the helicopter. Kristina noticed and extended her hand out to assist with the protections. Ribbons of blinding blue energy shot out and circled around us.

"Baylor," Brickson said, "I'm deferring to you here. I want to save this girl, but if you know we're entering into something dangerous, then we need to turn back."

"We're almost there!" I yelled. "We can't turn back now."

"This ain' a pretty sight, Baylor," Charlie bellowed from the entrance.

I looked out the window, and between the spotlight and the moon, I could see the trouble we were approaching. Just ahead, an eerie green mist billowed just above the waves, as the Lost Souls—a mixture of Ashens and morphing dark spirits—drifted ominously, slowly, waiting for their prey.

Suddenly an Ashen flew past the helicopter, and the power seemed to sputter.

"Baylor!" yelled a voice from outside. "Kristina!"

It was Archie, caught in the Ashen's grasp.

"No!" Kristina yelled, blasting blue energy at the Ashen, but missing it. It swerved back toward us, its billowy, misshapen figure blending in with the dark sky. Luckily its eyes, burning green and vicious, helped to pinpoint its precise location. Colonel Fleetwood jumped from the windshield and, in a brilliant flash of light, speared the demon through its gut.

It let out a wretched scream, comprised of the agony of one thousand mourning mothers, released Archie, and hurtled back down to rejoin its fellow lost souls. Two more immediately shot up to take the wounded demon's place.

"We'll never be able to fight them all off to save Helena in time," the colonel shouted through the entrance before turning back around to battle the demons. He slashed at the demons, which took swipes at both him and the helicopter, and we jerked violently.

"Baylor," Dad said, "are we in danger? What's going on?"

Charlie was looking sadly down at Helena on top of the overturned boat, just next to Archie's dead body.

"I worked on a boat for years and years," he said softly. "I've heard stories about the mysterious

disasters at sea. I know what these things can do." He
didn't seem to be talking to me and Kristina. "They
won' stop attacking until they get their soul." He
chuckled softly. "Luckily they're not too picky. Any
soul'll do."

"Kristina," the colonel shouted, "there's a third
one coming. I need backup!"

"Charlie?" Kristina said, ignoring the colonel, her
tone panicked.

"I can't let 'em take her," he said. "It can' go like
that." He turned to us, his lopsided form highlighted
from the shaking of the helicopter.

"Kristina!" the colonel shouted. The helicopter
shook just then; the lights flickered, and the sharp
pull in the pit of my stomach indicated we lost a few
feet of altitude.

"Baylor!" Dad and Brickson shouted simultane-
ously.

"Charlie, no," Kristina shrieked. "We can figure it
out."

"Baylor, can you hear me?" Dad shouted.

"Hold on," I shouted.

"An O'Brien man must do what he must do," Charlie
said. He nodded to us, his face resolute, and he turned
around and jumped out the entrance into the swarm of
Lost Souls below.

The colonel, busy fighting the demons, didn't notice him fall until it was too late. "What are you doing, Charlie?!" he shouted. "Come back!"

Immediately the spirits circled him, like a deranged flock of pigeons fighting over the biggest, freshest bread crumb ever. The two that Colonel Fleetwood had been fighting joined the feasting, and he returned seconds later, his expression stunned.

"He just sacrificed his eternal soul for the girl," he said. "He'll be at their mercy forever, unable to cross back into the Beyond. I'm not sure I've ever met anyone that brave."

"We can't let it be in vain," Kristina said, still eyeing the Lost Souls. "That'll keep them at bay for only so long. Baylor, do you have matches?"

"Of course!"

"Your amulet," she said. "Take it off, light it on fire, and drop it into the mist."

"Don't I need it for protection?" I asked. "Especially here?"

"If this thing's as strong as I think it is, we should be safe for the time being."

I pulled the amulet off my neck, took out my box of matches, and struck one live.

"Baylor!" Brickson yelled. "Are you crazy? Put that out! You can't light that in here!"

"I can if it saves our lives," I said. I touched the flame to the amulet, which caught fire beautifully, like a miniature sun, and looked at Kristina. "Ready?" I asked.

"Do it!"

I chucked it out the open door, and the colonel brandished his burning white sword. He sliced at the amulet and batted it toward the frenzied feeding demons below. Kristina, watching it fall for several seconds, took aim and shot her blue energy into the mist.

TIP
22
UPDATE: Amulets are *fantastic* at keeping bad spirits away. (Still bad for blending in, though.)

"SPREAD THE LIGHT," SHE MUTTERED.

And a fusion bomb of energy went off below, followed by the unnatural hisses and groans of dozens of Lost Souls—the newer, weaker ones being eviscerated, and the older, stronger ones fleeing. Moments later the mist dissipated, the helicopter stopped sputtering, and the path to rescuing Helena was clear.

Kristina looked pleased but she wasn't smiling. "I hope any that got away slowly and painfully decompose into nothing."

The colonel looked at her somberly. "Charlie will be remembered for all eternity for his bravery."

"We have visuals on the boat," Brickson said, shaking his head. "Unbelievable. All the data, for nothing. You ready to go down, Monty?"

As Monty was lowered down on a line to rescue Helena, Archie went back down to be with her too. He seemed to regret his choice with the spotlight shining over his body, though.

"Yikes," he said materializing next to us. "I look rough."

"Yeah," Kristina said, "ghosts don't normally like to hang out near their bodies for a reason."

"Because the body starts to look like a blistered toe?"

"Something like that," she said.

We watched in silence as the rescuer secured Helena and was lifted back up to the helicopter. She was unconscious, and Brickson went to work on her, taking her vitals, hooking her up to an IV, and assessing her body for injuries. Meanwhile, the rescuer went down again to collect Archie's body. It was an eerie scene as the helicopter hovered over his body, the rotor's force creating a small storm in the waters below, the powerful spray hitting my face.

"What do you remember about the day you went

missing?" Kristina asked Archie, trying to distract him from the retrieval.

"Feeling totally out of control," he said. "We weren't supposed to take the boat out—I'd actually promised my dad I wouldn't—but Helena really wanted to go for a cruise, so I agreed, thinking it would only be for thirty minutes or so."

"Oh no," Kristina said, grimacing. "Breaking a promise is the textbook example of bad karma. It makes people extremely vulnerable to dark influences, and your situation was that much worse being on open water with some Lost Souls lurking nearby. I'm guessing you lost control of the boat pretty quickly?"

"It was like we got caught in a tornado or something," he said, his eyes wide. "Everything went topsy-turvy, we were flailing all over the place, and next thing we know, we're stranded in the middle of nowhere. I honestly thought we would be rescued in just a few hours. We hadn't gone that far from shore."

"And then no one came for you?"

"Yep. And hours turned to days, except I had no concept of day or night because I felt like I began to lose my mind."

She nodded. "I think you did a little bit. The dreams of the dying are said to have special properties; I think that's one reason you were able to communicate with Baylor."

"You knew I was dying?"

She looked embarrassed. "I suspected it."

"Is that why you looked so sad when we first met?"

She frowned. "I didn't mean to look sad. I just couldn't help but feel like I knew what was going to happen to you, and I didn't think it was fair."

"Well, you turned out to be right."

"Unfortunately."

Helena was shocked for a number of reasons when she finally came to.

First, the confirmation that Archie was dead.

Second, the mere fact she was alive at all—she'd been convinced she was going to die on that boat.

Third, the news that a boy medium named Baylor Bosco had aided in her search-and-rescue. She had no memory of me. My conversations with her had only been part of Archie's dreams.

Her parents were equally shocked to discover that it was their darling daughter who'd been the one to want to take the boat out. They'd been so convinced it was Archie; the thought it may have been Helena had never crossed their minds.

I wasn't there for any of these revelations, though.

I found out the personal stuff from a few phone calls with Helena and her parents in the days that followed, and many other details I'd learned on the news. My face was, once again, plastered across the news stations; this time I was being touted as a national hero.

That title was ridiculous, but it did help me out with Jack.

His friends, though still scarred from the experience at the house, seemed to think it was cool that I'd helped find those two lost kids that had been all over the news.

Jack had invited them over again, and they'd agreed—but not at night. They'd stick to hanging out at the Bosco residence during the daytime. I thought that was a fair compromise.

I no longer had the amulet, which Kristina didn't see as a problem at all.

"It was never meant to be permanent, anyway," she said as we walked home from school, "and I can't help but think it did more harm than good."

"But we were able to save Helena with it *and* destroy those demons."

"That's true," she said, "but I can't shake a feeling." She furrowed her brows. "I've been thinking so much about it. Archie's dying dreams were one reason why you might have connected with him, but that can't be the only reason. There are a lot of dying people in the world, and you don't talk to all of them in your dreams." She looked at me side-eyed. "At least, not that you tell me about."

"I don't!"

"It might sound crazy, but what if the stone retained some of the Bruton's negative energy, and that's what connected us to Archie, Helena, and the Lost Souls?"

"Could that be true?" Something tickled my hair, and I looked up. A light flurry of snow was dropping from the sky. The first of the season. "Are you sure?"

"I don't think so," she said, her voice ominous. "But it's a much better option than the alternatives."

"It is?" I said, semihorrified. "What else do you suspect?"

She shook her head. "I need to do some more investigating before I worry you."

"Let it go," I said, putting my hoodie up.

"No point in fussing over it," Archie said. He'd been joining us over the last week as he got his bearings on the other side. "What's done is done. And regardless, you're not responsible for what those bad spirits do."

"I know that," she said. "I'm just still think about

the visit from Adam and Minh's relatives. I can't help but feel like things are changing, Baylor. For both of us."

With the amulet gone, I couldn't walk around dreams as easily anymore, which Kristina didn't think was such a bad thing. I didn't disagree with her, but I still wanted to be able to check in on people; which is to say, I wanted to be able to spy on Aiden and see how he was doing.

However, it didn't seem too necessary. Ever since he recovered J's purse from the mysterious masked bandit—and heard J fawn about it anyone who'd listen—he'd been acting with more confidence. I like to think the new dream catcher also had something to do with it—perhaps it actually catch those bad feelings, in addition to nosy friends. He still couldn't look J in the eye without experiencing a momentary full-body panic, but even baby steps were still steps in the right direction.

Kristina also explained I could still technically dreamwalk even without the amulet. "The trick is recognizing you're in the dream," she said. "It might take some practice, but you'll get there. It took forever to learn how to tune out spirits, but you managed to do that."

I groaned thinking of the effort that took. Years and years of work. I didn't want to repeat it. "Can't we just make a new amulet? Maybe something a bit more subtle this time?"

"We're discussing it," she said. "Luckily the holidays are approaching, and all the light and positivity will act as natural protections for you."

"A demon-free Christmas," I said. "What more could I ask for?"

"I don't know," she said, lightly, "maybe a girlfriend?"

"Ouch," said Archie.

TIP

23

Believe in yourself.

BAYLOR BOSCO: NATIONAL HERO OR NATIONAL SHAME?

Self-proclaimed medium Baylor Bosco has done it again. He's dominated headlines recently, fooling people into believing he single-handedly saved Helena Papadopoulos, the fourteen-year-old Florida girl who'd been missing for a week. Her friend Archie Perceval died while awaiting rescue.

But what if it were to be revealed that there was more to the story?

What if not everything was as it seemed?

Stay tuned for a special series about Baylor Bosco's exploits, coming up soon.

—Carla Clunders, editor-at-large,

NewEnglandRealNews.net

"Hi, Carla? This is Baylor Bosco."

"Oh, hello there, Baylor. I was wondering if you'd call."

"That's nice. Listen, I don't really care what you're planning since your website is an embarrassing sham, but I just want you to know one thing: If you talk about any of my family or friends, I will come after you."

"You'll come after me?"

"That's right, in the same way that you're coming after me, except I'd actually have a reason."

"Oh, I have my reasons, Mr. Bosco."

"Care to enlighten me?"

"They're very personal, as you may have guessed."

"Well, if it helps at all, I'm genuinely sorry for anything I may have done to hurt you."

Cough.

"And I hope you can find it in your heart to forgive me."

"Get off your high horse. You're only saying that so I won't publish articles about you anymore."

"Well, you're not wrong, but I also would never intentionally hurt someone, unlike you. Tell me, just how long did it take you to hack into Archie and Helena's hotline voice mail to dig up that information?"

"I have no idea what you're talking about," she said, her voice velvety.

"I'm going to hang up now, Carla. Remember what I said."

I'd tried sounding brave on the phone, but my heart was pounding the entire time, and my mouth had felt so dry I'd swallowed, like, eighteen times.

"Think it worked?" Kristina asked.

"Who knows," I said, "but honestly, if she doesn't listen to me, I meant what I said."

"What are you going to do about it?" she asked.

"Have you looked at the message boards online recently?" I asked.

"On which website?" In the last week, a new one had sprung up: ImABayliever.com.

"That's my point," I said, though my cheeks still burned. "I've got a whole army of Baylievers"——my ears felt like they were on fire, I hated saying the word—"at my disposal. If Carla doesn't listen, I'll unleash the hounds."

"Sounds exciting," said Kristina. "It's nice you're embracing your fans."

"I wouldn't go that far," I said, "but if they're willing to help out . . ."

I got ready for bed shortly afterward—threatening someone over the phone really takes it out of you.

I drifted off to sleep, finding myself back in the wide-open field with the brilliant colorful sky beaming overhead. I walked down the field and saw Mr. Moose sitting cross-legged, top hat balanced on antlers, sipping tea from fine china.

"Lovely to see you again, Mr. Moose," I said. "It's been a while."

He bowed, offering me a cup of tea.

"I haven't seen you since . . . ," I began to say as I reached for the cup. And it clicked into place—I was dreaming! I hadn't seen him since I entered Bobby's dream for the first time last week.

"I've gotta go, Mr. Moose!" I said, running up the hill toward the light as the moose stared after me and shook its head, its arm still outstretched with the cup of tea.

I somersaulted back onto Loved Ones' Lane and

admired all the shooting stars. I didn't really have the urge to visit anyone; it was just nice knowing I was connected to all my loved ones this way.

I turned left down the path, the way I'd been going for the last week, and looked at all the shooting stars. Who were these people? I'd only explored a handful of the doors. I had a long way to go, but I had plenty of time. It'd be easy to devote more time to dream-walking without having to worry about Archie's dreams at the end of the lane.

I reached the edge, where the ocean used to roar below, and sighed.

At least we saved Helena. Poor Archie didn't make it, but dang it, we got Helena back.

I was about to turn and head to my door to dream when I spotted it in the distance—the rectangular door again.

It seemed so far away today, but I was curious, and really, I had nothing else to do except go to sleep. So I leaped into the black nothing and glided forward. This must have been what floating through outer space felt like; I tumbled gently, spinning and flipping and somersaulting my way to the rectangle, the edges of which grew brighter and more intense as I moved closer.

And after what seemed like an hour, I made it. The

light was practically bursting at the seams, making the door bulge out. It seemed like if I just tapped it, it might be in danger of blasting open and unleashing its contents into dream space.

I reached for the handle, noticing a funny vibration, a funny kind of pull, like my hand and the handle were both magnets of the same charge, resisting each other. I pushed through and grasped it, throwing it open.

The most dazzling, mesmerizing bright white light flooded my body with warmth, and just as I was about to peek my head in, a sudden force knocked me backward. A million blue sparks exploded around me, and I zoomed back into my bed and woke up with a heavy gasp, like I was sucking my soul back into my body.

The lights flicked on, and surrounding my bed were Kristina, Colonel Fleetwood, and some other ghosts I didn't recognize—one was a dark-skinned man wearing a colorful set of silky robes; another was a stern Asian woman who was looking me up and down, over and over; and the last one, with about 99 percent certainty, was Albert Einstein, complete with the flyaway white hair, thick mustache, and friendly-but-perplexed smile.

"How did you just do that, Baylor?" Kristina shouted, her voice quivering.

"Do what?" I asked.

She and Fleetwood exchanged horrified glances.

"Baylor, you nearly entered the Beyond," Kristina said, throwing her arms out.

Her words didn't land the dramatic blow she'd been aiming for.

I just shrugged and said, "So? What's the big deal? Who are these people?" I was eyeing the Einstein twin, wanting solid confirmation as to whether I should be filled with excitement or not.

"They're not important right now! How did you get to that door?"

"It kept showing up last week during Archie's dreams," I said.

"During his dying dreams," she said, confused. "And you still have access to it now? Something's wrong. Only ghosts can enter the Beyond. If you had moved forward another inch . . . you would have been stuck there forever."

I scoffed. "How do you know that? Has someone actually tested that?"

"Baylor, you don't seem to understand the gravity of what I'm trying to tell you."

"I do understand what you're saying, but I'm also reminding you that you're the one who always says there are no set rules."

Albert Einstein (or his most seasoned imposter)

nodded in agreement, and a frisson of excitement passed through my body. I was trying not to freak out in case it was him. Had I just made a point that the smartest guy to ever live agreed with?

"Well, this is the exception to that rule, then," Kristina said.

"You're just repeating what someone else told you," I said. "You don't actually know whether I'd get stuck there or not."

"Don't ever open that door again, Baylor," she said, pointing at me with her index finger, a flare of blue energy escaping from the tip. "In fact, don't ever go near it again."

I rolled my eyes. "I hear you. I'll avoid it from now on."

"I can't tell whether you're being serious," she said, "but I'm telling you now: If you go through that door, you'll never come back out of it."

I nodded. "I understand."

But I couldn't help but feel she was wrong. I could communicate with dead people and see demons and make talismans and amulets. I could see memories attached to random objects. I could walk through people's dreams and save the life of someone hundreds of miles away. And no matter how worried Kristina was, I could surely walk through a door to the Beyond and live to tell the tale.

Acknowledgments

ALL MY LOVE AND THANKS GOES TO MY parents for their never-ending support. Love you, Mom and Dad. Ben, Jenny, and Colin—you guys are all right, too, I guess. Love ya.

A huge thank-you to the rest of my wonderful family. So many of you have shown me immense love and support, and I truly appreciate it. The same sentiment goes to my friends, who've listened to me blabber on about the books and put up with me skipping various activities thanks to writing, editing, etc. But just look at this beautiful book you're holding—it was all worth it!

Special shout-out to Dan Lazar for being such an awesome, hardworking agent, and to everyone else at Writers House, especially Torie Doherty-Munro. My editor, Amy Cloud, deserves endless praise and thanks for her diligence in shaping and shepherding this book through the editorial process. Thanks to everyone else at Simon & Schuster, especially Audrey Gibbons, Karin Paprocki, and Mara Anastas.

About the Author

ROBERT IMFELD is the author of *Baylor's Guide to the Other Side* and *Baylor's Guide to Dreadful Dreams*. He grew up in Orlando, Florida, and like any self-respecting Floridian, he split his free time evenly between the beach and Disney World. After graduating from the University of Florida, he put his journalism degree to good use by saving lives at a luxury resort (some call this "lifeguarding") in Orlando, interning/ brewing coffee at a production company in LA, and managing finances for country songwriters in Nashville. He now lives in New York City, where he works in marketing by day and writes kids' books by night.

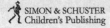

FOLLOW THE CLUES.
CRACK THE CODE. STAY ALIVE.

EBOOK EDITIONS ALSO AVAILABLE

ALADDIN
SIMONANDSCHUSTER.COM/KIDS